The Martini Club Mystery

Alan Eysen

The Martini Club Mystery
by Alan Eysen

...

ISBN-10: 0-9976761-5-9
ISBN-13: 978-0-9976761-5-0

Seven Es, LLC
Mount Pleasant, SC

Distributed by Bublish, Inc.

Cover Artwork by Berge Design

To the stalwart members of The Martini Club, who inspired this book with their wit, wisdom and libation.

1
Flying

Jay Corrigan flew lazy circles over the Parrot's Caw subdivision. The sky was azure blue; the golf course below a winding strip of brilliant green. This was the time the retired airline pilot had been waiting for—no schedules, no responsibilities, just the pure joy of making lazy circles in the sky.

The tiny two-seat Cessna 152 responded instantly to Corrigan's touch. He was hands-on flying in this little high-winged bird. He and the plane were one body linked by touch. Corrigan no longer was managing a computer-driven commercial plane, responsible for hundreds of passengers. He was just having fun.

Oops, he thought, remembering he did have one responsibility today. He had promised the Parrot's Caw Property Owners Association that he would take photographs of the fifteen-hundred-acre development, with its thirty miles of roads and drains, its seventy-five drainage ponds, its twenty-plus miles of walking and biking trails, and many acres of carefully trimmed flowers, bushes and trees. The association board had requested the photos as part of its preparation for negotiations with the property's developer.

Yet he hesitated.

Instead of shooting photos, he climbed to thirty-five hundred feet to get a more panoramic view of the area. There was Parrot's Caw, a complex of more than two thousand homes, town homes and condominiums. Its residents were upper middle class, mostly a mixture of successful businessmen and professionals—doctors, lawyers, accountants and engineers. Of course, he had met some offbeat souls, retired college professors, an ex-CIA operative, even a former journalist. Good folks to drink with.

The neighborhood's manicured lawns, landscaped gardens and rolling golf course painted a sharp contrast to what Corrigan saw when he looked to the southeast. There, he spotted a distinctly different neighborhood. It was made up mostly of rundown shanties and mobile homes sitting on concrete blocks. Poor blacks lived there. He could make out several of them riding bikes on the slender, two-lane roads—*not for the exercise*, he thought, *but because they can't afford cars.*

To the south lay the city of Stuarton, known to many as The Miracle City because the colonial seaport town had survived a British siege and blockade during the Revolutionary War by trickery as much as grim determination. Its militiamen intermixed real and artificial cannons on their ramparts to give a more formidable appearance and poked numerous unmanned rifles out of windows and over parapets to further the impression of a greater number of defenders. Some of their dead were propped up behind these weapons to add authenticity. After weeks of bombardment, the British fleet withdrew rather than test Stuarton's defenses further by landing troops.

Today, Stuarton residents were largely middle class, earning their living from small businesses that catered either to the tourist trade or the sale of farm products. A small section was filled with venerable mansions, some still occupied by the heirs of their original builders. Most of these architectural jewels, however, were now in the hands of successful entrepreneurs and celebrities who enjoyed a certain anonymity among Stuarton's polite, look-the-other-way citizenry.

Flying in a slow turn to the north, Corrigan was able to peer out his window far to the west. There he saw miles of farms and small ranches. *Damn*, he thought, *I think I see some cattle and real cowboys down there. Now it's time to play*. With that, he pushed the throttle in to full power and pulled the control wheel into his gut. The Cessna's engine roared as its nose pointed straight up to the sky. For a tantalizing moment, the plane remained motionless, stalled, as if hung on an invisible string. Then, its left wing dropped precipitously, and the plane began to spin— slowly at first, then more rapidly. It looked to Corrigan as if the earth, not the plane, was spinning more and more rapidly as it rose up toward him. He laughed, shoved the control wheel forward, leveled the wings, pressed hard on the right rudder and reduced power. As the spin stopped, he eased off the right rudder and gently pulled back on the control wheel, putting the plane back in level flight. *Fun's over.* The altimeter indicated he had lost 150 feet.

He turned back to the southeast toward Parrot's Caw and began a slow descent. He reached for his camera, an old German Leica, banked the plane over to a forty-five-degree angle, and began shooting. By the time he tied down the little rental plane, he was ready for a drink. *Where the hell are Brady, Smyth and Ginsberg when you need them?*

2
In the Beginning

MANY OF BRODY Brady's personal daily rituals were the result of his creative imagination. There was, for example, his Tuesday and Thursday walking schedule. On those two days, Brady wore a towel around his neck and a headband that said FEDERER. He would start his walks at precisely 10:00 a.m., which allowed him to reach his halfway point, the development's tennis courts, a half hour later. This coincided with the conclusion of the regular women's doubles tennis matches. Brady would offer his towel to any attractive lady who seemed in need of such assistance. Soon the players expected Brady to arrive, and some struck up an acquaintance with "that charming man."

On Wednesdays, Brady would borrow his neighbor's Yorkshire Terrier for a walk. He had learned that women were attracted to small, fluffy dogs. Though the Yorkie was a male named Brute, on their walks Brady called him Lover Girl. A heavy coat of hair concealed the distinguishing male member until the dog was picked up to be cuddled. This made for lengthy conversations with women concerning male and female anatomy. After each walk, Brady returned the dog promptly to its owner, borrowing it off schedule only if a Yorkie-loving woman decided to pay him a personal visit.

Mondays and Fridays were set aside for what Brady called "conversation walks," strolls with a special group of men more or less his age. He was seventy-eight. All the men invited on these walks were bright, well educated, mostly retired, and above all interesting. They also shared a kindred taste for martinis.

The Brady walkers, as they began calling themselves, met at the entrance to the Parrot's Caw Clubhouse, an English Tudor structure that fed and lubricated golfers, pinochle players and those interested in spending a day away from their spouses. It was after one such conversation walk that The Martini Club was born. To say it was formally created would be an overstatement. Best to say it simply evolved from a discussion between Brady and Nathan Ginsberg on the merits of drinking, and their inability to do so while walking.

Ginsberg was slightly younger than Brady, and could discuss anything from philosophy to baseball scores with wit and wisdom. He was tall, nearly as tall as Brady. Unlike Brady, though, Ginsberg was broad shouldered and muscular with a perpetual three days growth of beard. He could have passed for one of those mature male models featured in erectile dysfunction commercials.

"What I admire about you, Nathan," Brady said, "is that you can hold your liquor so well. In my ethnic persuasion, that would be considered a badge of honor. In yours, probably not so much."

"True, especially since I am a rabbi."

"A rabbi?" Brady responded in disbelief. "During my days in Washington, I ran into lots of Jews who could drink with the best, but none of them was a rabbi."

"A heavy drinking Jew is the quintessential assimilationist. If he can drink like a goy, he can pass for a goy, so deep is the Jewish inferiority complex," Ginsberg replied. "But passing for a goy doesn't work well in the rabbi business. Congregations want rabbis not only to be Jewish, but to look Jewish and smell Jewish. That means, horseradish on your breath...yes; liquor on your breath... no. Fortunately, I am retired. I took up drinking after my working years. All that being said, there is precedence for having a drunken leader in the Bible."

"Is this going to be a sermon on the virtues of drinking?" Brady asked in expectation of some witty Talmudic offering. "Being of Irish heritage and having labored in some of the best bars in D.C., I can say I need no conversion."

"In your case, no conversion, just a little Jewish perspective," Ginsberg responded. "I think you already understand the sins and virtues of alcohol. In Genesis, God decides he doesn't like the life He has created on earth with Adam and Eve, so He tries again. He floods the world, and drowns everybody except for one righteous man, his family and a bunch of animals—there is some dispute as to their number—but in the end, all are saved, and life begins again on this lonely planet."

"Touching. So what's the point?"

"The point is this: the one righteous man He picks to lead the little band of start-overs is a vintner named Noah. Immediately after he finds dry land, what does Noah do?"

"I know." Brady responded with a wink. "He lets all those creatures off the ark to go copulate."

"My question was rhetorical, smart guy. The Bible says, 'And Noah, the farmer, began and planted a vineyard. And he drank of the wine and was drunken.' Things get a little sloppy after that, but Noah lived nine hundred and fifty years and started a whole line of descendants, including you and me. My point is that if it weren't for a drunken pre-Jew, none of us would be here."

"Hallelujah," replied Brady. "And that explains why Jesus turned water into wine. He just wanted to keep the party going."

Before Ginsberg could reply, Gerald Smyth joined them with a healthy clap on both their backs. "So boys, what are we going to argue about today?"

It was then that Brady had an epiphany. "The three of us love to drink martinis, tell wild stories and argue about everything from politics to women. Why don't we meet at each other's homes instead of on the street, so we can imbibe while we altercate? The host will supply the martinis and some food. We can call it The Martini Club. Each of us can bring in an additional member as long as he is a kindred spirit."

"There must be only one rule," Ginsberg responded, "that there are no rules, no passwords, no secret handshakes or special number cards with our faces on them, nothing that will bring order out of the chaos we are seeking."

"Agreed," Smyth said.

"Whoa," Brady objected. "You have suggested a rule that cannot be put in place unless there are rules for voting a rule in or out of place. Without such formative rules, there can be no way to adopt primal rules for barring rules."

"I would suggest that does not have to be the case," Ginsberg countered. "The religious and scientific laws that govern us did not require an a priori mechanism to put them in place. These laws are givens. They are inherent to the universe, like gravity and magnetism. God made them all out of nothing, a void."

"Are you, rabbi, suggesting that God created gravity and magnetism?" asked Brady.

"Yes, exactly. Science can't explain what set this all in motion. I am suggesting that God is our convenient name for the universality that put all these laws in place without benefit of outside jurisdiction or requirement of a majority vote. When Moses stood before the burning bush and asked God his name, God answered, 'I am what I am,' or as the Greeks translated it 'I will be what I will be.' How much more universal can you get? How can that be challenged?"

Smyth raised a large, hard hand, silencing the debaters. "Enough," he cried. "It is clear we are standing atop Mount Sinai at this very moment—though there isn't a hill in sight—and we have just received revealed truth. The Martini Club has been called forth as a revelation. The first meeting will be held at my place within the week."

The Martini Club was born and grew to ten members, each bringing a special personality and branch of knowledge to the assemblage—the theater arts and fine arts, politics, business, aviation, journalism, espionage, sex and psychology.

3
Brody Brady

SAM GRIEGER'S FIRST encounter with the manipulations of Brody Brady came as he was unpacking boxes and placing items where his wife Sheila had dictated—dishes in the cabinets near the refrigerator, toaster oven on the counter near the coffee maker, automatic can opener to be screwed into the base of the cabinet overhanging the dishwasher. *If I let my mind go blank*, he thought, *I won't remember that I failed shop in high school and that my teacher called me tool disadvantaged. I have twisted myself like a circus contortionist into the twenty-two inches between the dishwasher and the overhanging cabinet and am trying to rotate screws into remarkably hard wood.*

Someone began aggressively banging on the front door.

"Who is it?" Grieger called.

"Your neighbor, Brody Brady. It's an emergency."

"Hold on a minute."

"I don't have a minute. It's an emergency."

"What's the emergency?"

"I'm bleeding."

"Hold on." Grieger untwisted himself carefully off the dishwasher, mindful that his skull could be penetrated at any moment by partially driven steel screws.

He opened the door to see Brody Brady looking like a gaunt parody of the Statue of Liberty, right hand held high, wrapped in a towel sodden with blood. As a retired newspaper reporter, Grieger had seen his fill of bloody bodies, but Brody Brady looked different. *Probably because he's still alive.* "I'll call 911."

"No time for 911," Brady replied. "Do you have some large bandages?"

"Yes, somewhere in one of these boxes," Grieger answered, pointing at a hallway filled with half-opened boxes. "My wife would know where, but she isn't home."

"Then you will have to do. Start going through the boxes," Brady commanded.

Grieger began rummaging through them without success. He looked up to see Brady dripping blood. "You are bleeding on my boxes and on my new parquet floor," Grieger shouted.

"I don't want to bleed on your boxes and floor, so get me some bandages quickly," Brady snapped back.

In desperation, Grieger grabbed Brady by his blood tipped arm and rushed him to the kitchen sink. *At least now he won't bleed to death on my new floor.* He pulled away the blood soaked towel revealing a gash that ran from Brady's middle finger, across his palm nearly up to his wrist. "This needs stitches. A bandage won't do it," Grieger said, trying to feign compassion.

Grieger recalled the cops slipping on plastic gloves and booties before touching the victims of mob hits. *What if this guy has AIDs or hepatitis? Am I going to die from a horrible disease I haven't even derived in some perverse pleasure?* Aloud, he said, "Why don't you go to the emergency room? There's a hospital nearby. I'll drive you."

"I can't go," Brady replied. "See the 18-wheeler down at the end of the block. It's full of my stuff. They're unloading it into my place right now. I have to tell them where to put things."

"I still think you should go to the emergency room. Just let them dump the furniture wherever. My wife will be home soon, and I'll tell her to tell the movers where to put things. She knows that sort of stuff. She puts things in all the right places. Her mother taught her."

"She doesn't know where I want to put my things, nor does her mother," Brady responded, agitation creeping into his voice.

"Sheila has great instincts about that kind of stuff," Grieger replied knowingly. "It's in women's genes. When we lived in caves, they put all the rocks in all the right places. That's how we learned to sit down. By the time we come back from the emergency room everything will be right where it should be."

"No," Brady replied resolutely. "I will stay with my furniture to the end, even if I bleed to death and it's your fault."

Grieger realized his situation was hopeless. Brady was prepared to die just to make sure his furniture was properly placed, and would blame him with his dying breaths. He rushed to the closet and grabbed a large beach towel emblazoned with the image of a very large crab. He twisted it around Brady's wound and secured it with several turns of packing tape. The flow of blood was slowed but not stopped.

"You are still bleeding," Grieger said hopelessly.

"I take Coumadin. It's a blood thinner. You see, I have a bad heart," Brady explained like some patient teacher. "It's very hard to stop the bleeding."

"I think we should go to the emergency room," Grieger answered.

"I'm already scheduled to go in tomorrow for some minor heart surgery. I'll have them stitch up my hand at the same time, a kind of two for one," Brady countered, smiling.

"Heart surgery tomorrow?" Grieger questioned, no longer surprised at his neighbor's answers. "I don't think they combine such things."

"I'll talk to them," Brady said confidently. "I can be quite persuasive. Besides, I have Medicare. It's all covered."

Grieger knew Brady had won. It was time to soldier on. Grieger marched him to the door. "Keep your arm elevated. As soon as my wife gets back we'll find some real bandages and bring them over to your place," he said. "By the way, how'd you get this cut?"

"They were bringing in a case of my very good wine, and they dropped it. I reached inside the case to check the damage and was stabbed by a bottle of Argentine Malbec," Brady replied with a grin.

"What a waste of good wine," Grieger sympathized, smiling back.

"I knew I'd like you," Brady answered as he left, towel and hand held high.

And thus their friendship began.

4
The Chant

THE NEXT TIME Sam Grieger saw Brody Brady was at the get-to-know you meeting of the newly formed Parrot's Caw Condominium Owners Association, or PCCOWA, as it came to be known. The event was held in an all-purpose ballroom at the development's central building, quaintly called The Domain. The ballroom itself was named The Dunk since it also served as a basketball court. The backboards were pulled up on this occasion, serving as anchors for the strings attached to large red, white and blue balloons that caromed off the coffee-colored ceiling. Periodically, they would snag on the folded hoops and make gaseous sounds as they pulled free. Their flatulence was overwhelmed now by the powerful voice of Chris Bideau, the property manager and developer's son.

"I personally want to thank each of you for being the first settlers in a row of unique condominium structures that RB&S Homes hopes to fill with comfortable retirees from the north, just like yourselves." Recalling his religious education at Goodness of God College, he added, "You are on the frontier of the Promised Land. Thanks to RB&S Homes, you have at long last escaped the cold, the shoveling of snow, the driving on ice, the wearing of heavy winter coats, the chill of icy winds and the huge heating bills...and you deserve it." Mixing his biblical geography, Bideau went on to proclaim, "You are no longer East of Eden. You are *in* Eden. Amen, brothers and sisters!"

His audience responded to his revival meeting oratory with polite applause, but not a single Hallelujah.

Unshaken, Chris Bideau switched to a more down-to-earth approach. "Each table has bottles of wine and delicious chocolate chip cookies. And there is more to come. We have chicken wings waiting in the kitchen oven and ice cream in the freezer."

Warming more to his master of ceremonies role, he added, "But before we get to the eating and drinking, RB&S Homes is going to treat you to something really special. We have created a Parrot's Caw chant," he shouted. "Chant it with me. It goes this way: PEE-SEE-SEE-OH-WHO-WAWA. The P not only stands for Parrot. It stands for perfect," he yelled into a crackling microphone. "Remember, accent on the first PEE and the WHO." He began rocking and rhythmically shouting:

PEE-SEE-SEE-OH-WHO-WA-WA.
PEE-SEE-SEE-OH-WHO-WA-WA.
PARROT'S CAW HAS ALL THE POW-WA.

A scantily dressed female, clearly wearing little or no underwear, jumped on the stage next to Bideau and began wiggling her bottom and waving pom-poms. She was slender, bosomy and pretty, but clearly years beyond her high-school cheerleading days.

"PEE-SEE-SEE-OH-WHO-WA-WA," she cheered. "C'mon, folks," she cried out. "Let's all join in."

Her low-cut top and mini skirt had awakened interest among the male condo owners. "Not since my high-school basketball days have I seen a wiggle like that," shouted a recently retired Wall Street lawyer sitting close to the stage. "But I left the cheering to the cheerleaders. I just tried to score—one way or the other." His remarks drew a round of applause and whistles from the men in the audience. His wife whacked his arm with her handbag.

Nobody joined in the chant. The pom-pom girl stopped wiggling.

"Ah, c'mon folks," a frustrated Chris Bideau pleaded into the microphone. "We're all on the same team here. We should have a cheer. We've got to have a cheer."

"We'd rather have the chicken wings," someone yelled from the back of the room.

Then Brody Brady jumped up. "In the meantime, why don't you let the young lady play some music and do some singing. I understand she's a got a great voice."

"Okay, okay," Chris Bideau responded, getting Brady's message. "RB&S Homes wants you to have a good time tonight." He signaled for the waiters to start bringing out the chicken wings. Turning to the pom-pom girl, he announced, "Get your other equipment on the stage, honey. It's time for you to entertain us." The girl quickly put two turntables, an amplifier and two speakers on the stage.

Bideau was about to hand her the microphone when a big man with a heavy beard walked in and shouted, "Hold it! She don't sing. She don't play music. She don't strip. And she don't wiggle, unless I say so. And I ain't said so, so I'm taking her home."

"Who are you?" Bideau asked.

"I'm her manager, her boss and her pimp," the big man said as he walked passed tables of gawking condo owners on his way to the stage.

"What the hell is going on, Brody?" Chris asked. "I thought you paid her."

"I did," Brady answered from his seat only a few feet away. Some heads turned toward him with curiosity, but most remained fixated on the big man in the T-shirt, leather vest and large tattooed arms as he headed toward the girl.

"Just a moment, sir," Bideau said as he stepped between the two. "If this is about money, we can straighten this out."

The big man stopped and looked at Chris, who at six feet four inches stood two inches taller than the big man and at two hundred and forty pounds was twenty pounds heavier.

"This ain't about money. The broad tried to go into business on her own. She needs to be taught a lesson," he said. He attempted to move around Bideau, but Bideau moved with him.

"Out of my way before I bust your skull," the big man said, pulling out a sharpened steel rod from a side pocket in his leather pants. Within seconds, Bideau smashed his knee into the thug's groin. As the big man doubled over, Bideau brought his right fist down on the back of his head, seized his right wrist in an iron grip and spun him around. The steel rod went flying. The bearded man screamed as his shoulder snapped, and he collapsed in a moaning heap on the floor. This would be the last thing the big man remembered before waking up in the Stuarton Hospital emergency room.

Bideau seized the microphone. "This is all some kind of misunderstanding, folks. Just stay seated and we'll go on with the evening. We still have ice cream sundaes coming." The image of sundaes didn't change the mood. The condo owners were streaming toward the doors.

The pom-pom girl was packing her equipment hastily and crying. "He'll kill me!"

"If he comes near you, tell him he'll answer to me," Bideau responded.

He saw Brody Brady leaving with the crowd. "Brady, we have to talk, now!"

Brady stopped and turned to face Bideau, who was stepping over the big man.

"You sold me on the chant. You sold me on the girl. You sold me on the night, Mr. Public Relations Man. And look what's happened. The condo owners are fleeing; some pimp tried to kill me, and I have to explain all this not only to the cops but also to my dad. I'm also out the five hundred bucks I paid you for your ideas and another two hundred and fifty for the cheerleader."

"They would have come around to chant after a few more glasses of wine and some dancing," Brady replied in a reassuring voice. As for the girl, I met her at a strip club downtown. She was pole dancing, playing music and singing. Seemed very talented, so I set her up with you. I didn't know we were supposed to go through her manager. You'd better call 911," Brady added as he headed for the door before Bideau decided to put him next to the big man.

5
Dear Old Dad

THE NEXT MORNING, Chris Bideau was still trying to understand what had occurred at the clubhouse. It was supposed have been the crowning touch on the creation of a suburban development aimed at the affluent fifty-five-and-over crowd. It was supposed to turn happy condominium owners into a word-of-mouth sales force that would help spur Parrot's Caw growth to hundreds of units in the next two years. Instead, it had turned into Wrestle Mania.

His daddy was especially angry. "You dumb bastard," Rufus Bideau hollered as he slammed Chris's head against the office wall. "How could you let that Brody Brady guy convince you to put on a side show that had a bitch and a bum ruin the evening? This was supposed to be a community-building event. Instead, I've had twenty calls from folks wanting to know whether they could sell their units back to us. On top of that, the cops want to talk to you about what happened."

"He was going to hit me with a steel pipe. I was only protecting myself," Chris protested in a hopeless defense.

"Personally, I would have shot the bastard," his daddy replied without sympathy. "Good thing I wasn't there. But how in the hell did you get mixed up with that bimbo?"

"Brady brought her to me. He told me he was a big-time public relations and advertising man from Washington, D.C., and he had this great idea to bring all the new condo owners together, create a community cheer and make them part of our sales force. All I had to do was pay him five hundred dollars to set things up. For another two hundred and fifty, he would get this cheerleader who could play music and sing."

"So you paid him seven hundred and fifty dollars to create a riot?" Rufus Bideau roared. "I'd slam your head against a wall one more time," he continued shouting, "but it wouldn't do any good! That Brady needs a lesson of his own on salesmanship."

After his daddy left the office, Chris sat in his chair and thought. *Maybe I'm not cut out for this sort of thing. What else could I have done? I wasn't about to let that guy smack me with a piece of steel. I tried to reason with him, even offered him money. Daddy probably would have shot the guy. And Lucas, well, he would have dragged him around the back and beat him to a pulp. And he would have enjoyed it.*

That's what Rufus Bideau liked most about Chris's older brother Lucas, the joy he expressed when being violent. It was a kind of release for him. Chris was as big and probably as strong as his brother, but derived little pleasure from intentionally hurting people. His daddy had unsuccessfully tried to correct this flaw in his youngest son.

Chris never forgot his introduction to Rufus's theory of life. He was seventeen. He had grown bigger, broader and more muscular and had been sent to the local supermarket to do the week's shopping.

When Chris returned, his daddy growled, "You forgot the milk and bread!" He slapped Chris hard across the face.

Chris felt a hot anger erupt, the culmination of absorbing thousands of such blows. He hurled his daddy against the wall, and watched him slide to the floor. The grocery bag his father was holding went flying. A bottle of chili sauce broke open, spattering his daddy with a thick, reddish brown goo. Rufus sat slumped motionless on the floor for a moment. Then, he reached inside his jacket, pulled out a pistol and aimed it at his son's chest. Chris stood frozen, waiting to be shot. He knew his daddy liked killing things. He'd seen him shoot people's pets when they came on his land.

"So you've got some piss and vinegar in you after all," he said lowering his weapon with a twisted, but forgiving smile. "Hand me a towel."

Chris grabbed a stained kitchen towel hanging from the oven's handle and gave it to his daddy. Rufus carefully wiped the chili sauce from his shirt. He stretched out his hand toward Chris. "Now help me up, boy." The youth grabbed his dad's hand and started to pull him to his feet. In a single motion, Rufus whipped out his pistol and smashed it against the side of his son's head, knocking him unconscious.

When Chris awoke, he looked up to see his daddy staring down at him. "You broke a fundamental rule of survival," Rufus Bideau said in a cold, controlled voice. "Don't ever give the other guy a break. No mercy, no forgiveness. You should have kicked me in the balls when you had the chance. Be angry and stay angry. It's the only true feeling. It will keep you alive."

Rufus never touched his youngest son again, but remained disappointed by him. Despite Rufus's relentless upbringing of the two boys, Chris never seemed to harden. Unlike Lucas, Chris was able to shrug off all the hurt and discipline. The boy somehow retained the character of his mother, a soft woman who had left Rufus years ago.

Chris, for his part, remembered happier times before his mother left. A time when his daddy threw those big arms around him in what he called his teddy bear hug. But one day, his dad went away, and when he came back the teddy bear hugs were gone. His mother was gone soon after. Chris had once mustered up the courage to ask why. "That's none of your damn business," was the reply. It was never discussed again. For Chris, all that was left was an ache, down deep inside. To this day, he never understood why his daddy had lost his capacity to love somewhere on a California mountaintop.

Despite his misgivings, Rufus saw some value in his soft son. Chris was smart. He had a certain charm and warmth. When properly honed, these characteristics would be of great advantage in the business jungle in which Rufus thrived. This was a world he knew contained two kinds of animals—wolves and sheep.

6
Finding God

Rufus Bideau was exhausted. As strong as he was, he had not anticipated the struggle he would have to endure climbing to the peak of Mt. Tyler, one of the highest peaks in California's Sierra Nevada Mountains. His powerful hands felt worn and limp inside his gloves. The thin air at thirteen thousand feet left him gasping with each breath. The biting cold, pushed by pulsating winds, sent shivers through his frame. It took all his willpower to maintain his senses. Yet, he was where he wanted to be—away from the world, his family, his possessions. He would remain in his tent, with his meager supplies, until the universal truth he had been seeking all his life was revealed to him.

He grew up in Stuarton—a small, southeastern city—the grandson of a part-time Christian missionary. He absorbed his grandfather's teachings and read his Bibles, old as well as new. He learned Greek, Hebrew and Aramaic so that he could understand the religious texts in their original tongues. In graduate school, Rufus studied Western religions. His doctoral thesis was considered brilliant. Despite all the degrees, all the research, and all the years of study, the same questions continued to torture him. What did life ultimately mean? What was its purpose? Did it even have a purpose? When confronted with Rufus's questions, his grandfather always returned to the same answer—the power of faith. "Have faith in our almighty God," he would say. "That is enough. God is beyond human understanding." For Rufus, that was not enough. God must in some way reveal the purpose of humanity.

Marrying and having children only temporarily diverted him from his nagging quest—that itch that could never be adequately scratched. He loved his wife and two sons, Lucas and Chris. Love was one of those unfathomable emotions. He had adopted it with the all the passion of a convert, bathing his family in it. But it was not an answer to his questions. It simply perpetuated humanity for its own self.

Then it struck him. Abraham took Isaac to Mount Moriah as a sacrifice to God. Moses ascended Mount Sinai to get his commandments. Jesus went up Mount Tabor to be transfigured and God's voice spoke to him as it had spoken to Abraham and Moses. Rufus suddenly realized that if he had any hope of hearing God's voice, and learning his true purpose on earth, he too must go up a mountain to find it. What better place to go than Mt. Tyler, named after a missionary like his grandfather, who sought to convert native Americans to Christianity.

Two months later, Rufus found himself half frozen at the top of the cold mountain. Around him were dozens of slabs of jutting black rocks. Snow fell periodically, creating a checkerboard landscape. For six days he sat. He waited. He endured. Then, on the seventh day, a dark, bearded figure approached him dressed in a heavy, black cloak. A hood hid all of his face, except for his piercing black eyes.

"Who are you?" Bideau asked.

"My name is Samyaza," the figure answered. "Why have you come to this mountain?"

"To find the purpose of life."

"That is simple. It has only the meaning you give it," the figure said.

"That is not enough. God knows its meaning, and He must tell me," Rufus Bideau protested. "Do you speak for God?"

"I am His watcher over humankind."

"Can you speak to the purpose of life?"

"Look for it in the constant struggle between the Sons of Light and the Sons of Darkness. Neither will emerge victorious, but in some distant time, they will merge and find in each other what they could not find in themselves. They will be something new. That is all there is—to forever become something new that will again be challenged."

"That is not enough!" Bideau stammered. "Are we merely condemned to go round and round and round? That is madness, and it does not explain why!"

"That is all human beings can expect to know," the stranger said, leaning on his staff.

Bideau felt anger rise in him like some hot flame. "Then you have told me nothing, old man!"

The figure remained serene. "I have told you all you can know, and have aroused in you the one emotion that ultimately drives all humanity—anger."

Then, the figure was gone.

A bright, white light shined down on Rufus's face. A man in a white coat looked down on him. "Oh, good, you are finally awake," he said. "It looks like you took a nasty fall. You broke your right leg badly. You were lucky the rangers found you or you might have frozen to death. What were you doing up there alone?"

"I was trying to find God."

7
Football

HARDLY HAD CHRIS Bideau tossed his cap into the sweaty air that blanketed the seven-hundred-forty-five black-robed graduates of Goodness of God College then his older brother, Lucas, tugged at him. "Boy, daddy has a job just waitin' for you. Between that fancy learning you got at GGC and that big body of yours, you will do just fine."

Chris's size and agility landed him a football scholarship to Goodness of God, where he excelled as a linebacker for three of his four years. In the beginning, he had loved to hit oncoming backs. Defensive Coach Moss Henderson pasted a special star on a defensive player's helmet every time he took an opponent out of the game. Five stars warranted a cash bonus. Chris's helmet was festooned with stars. He'd started a small bank account with the bonuses. But the hitting and hurting wasn't about the money. It was about pleasing his daddy. For a time, Rufus Bideau was pleased. "You showed 'em you had balls," his daddy once told him.

Affection turned to distaste in Chris's last season when he got hurt in a stunning collision with ULC's Archie Mayberry, a massive fullback on his way to the NFL. Mayberry got up, shrugged his shoulder pads and smiled while Chris rolled on the ground in agony. He had partially torn the stabilizer in his right knee, technically called the anterior cruciate ligament or ACL in sports jargon. As Chris writhed in pain on the field, Rufus got up from his stadium seat and left. He sought no information about his son's condition. In Rufus's mind Chris had been beaten, and losers didn't rate consideration.

Chris missed two games but returned from therapy just in time to face ULC's Mayberry again in a post-season bowl game. The clash was inevitable. Mayberry was going to go straight for Chris, if the chance came up. Mayberry knew the defensive back was hurt and figured he would want no part of a second collision. Mayberry knew that fear was a powerful weapon.

Mayberry got the call he wanted, a handoff to pick up three critical yards. A hole in the line opened. The only obstacle was Chris Bideau. Mayberry went straight at him. Mayberry didn't know that Chris wasn't afraid.

The two-hundred-seventy-pound fullback outweighed Chris by thirty pounds. As Mayberry charged forward, he thought he saw something in Chris's eyes, and it wasn't fear. *Hell, I'll carry that bastard over the fucking goal line, if he stays in my way.* He certainly had the strength to do it. Chris would just be some extra baggage. As the fullback's huge arm came up to swat Chris out of the way, Chris pivoted sharply, dipping his left shoulder just low enough to catch Mayberry's knees from behind. Using his low center of gravity, Chris drove hard into Mayberry's exposed joints. He felt Mayberry flip over his back and land with a deep grunt on the turf.

"You shit! Next time I'll bust your ass," Mayberry moaned from the ground.

"Nothing personal," Chris replied with a smile.

Defensive Coach Henderson, known to his players as The Wedge, was not a man for sophisticated hits. "You should have taken that boy head on and shown him who was the man in this house. That dancing around is nothing but pantywaist bullshit. We are playing football. We hit head on. We bang. We show them who is the man, so they don't come our way again...so they show respect. Respect is everything!"

The Wedge commanded little of the respect about which he preached. The team and most of its management long ago had concluded Henderson was the dumbest coach on the GGC staff. Some long gone quarterback had nicknamed him The Wedge, because it was one of the simplest tools known to man. The term became part of the college's vernacular. If a student was called "a wedge," it meant he was the stupidest kid around. If someone did something really dumb, he was said to have "wedged." But Coach Moss Henderson was the college president's brother-in-law, so he would be there as long as the president of GCC remained.

Chris was smart enough to know that as far as professional football was concerned, he was damaged goods. His take down of Mayberry came at a price—knee surgery. Chris enjoyed what was left of his senior year, screwing cheerleaders and tossing down beers with the guys.

It was hard not to like Chris Bideau. His face projected a good-looking innocence, abetted by pale blue eyes that twinkled with mischief, all topped by a shock of golden hair. His daddy, Rufus Bideau, knew these qualities would be assets to the family business.

8
The Boot

GERALD SMYTH SLUMPED in the old recliner that faced out into his spacious backyard. He was pleased to see that the Dok Champa, a Laotian white flower with a golden interior, was flourishing in his garden. To Laotians the flower meant joy in life and sincerity, hardly words that defined his experiences as a Central Intelligence Agency operative in that region. Yet the Dok Champa offered a kind of haven, and remained steadfastly beautiful, defying a world filled with ugly violence.

His CIA days were a distant memory. Now, he stood admiring the exotic flowers in the Parrot's Caw home he and his wife had purchased years ago as part of their retirement plan. It bordered a thick stand of woods that would give them the privacy they cherished. Unfortunately, his wife had died too soon to enjoy any of it. He often sat alone staring out the large glass doors at the rear of the house, enjoying the beautiful Southeast Asian flowers he so carefully cultivated in her memory.

"I did more good than bad, my love," Smyth said out loud to an empty house.

He thought back to the beginning of his career with the CIA. It was March of 1975. He had transitioned from the Army's Green Berets. Phipoc was his first CIA posting and possibly his last. It was a you-are-going-nowhere assignment. Officially, he was the Agricultural Attaché at the United States Consulate in Phipoc. Who'd even heard of tiny Phipoc, a principality wedged between Laos and Thailand? The war in Vietnam was winding down. North Vietnam had won. Nothing that happened in Phipoc—or Laos or Thailand for that matter—would change that inevitable fact.

His official assignment was to monitor the drug trade. Phipoc was a major transit point for the movement of opium and other narcotics through the Far East to Europe and the United States. The Agency, working with Army ground forces, would interdict this traffic based on information gathered by Smyth and others. Inside the consulate, he played an additional role—chief of security. In fact, he was the only security the consulate had aside from the two Marines assigned to guard the gates in front of the building.

The riot outside the consulate began around noon, shortly after word got out that a U.S. Army Special Forces unit had destroyed a drug storage warehouse used as a distribution center by local drug lords. Along with the loss of several million dollars in goods, three guards were killed and four others wounded. Even worse, fifty people were now out of work. The US Army's headquarters in Saigon acknowledged the attack, but argued that destruction of the warehouse was necessary—the drug lords were in reality Communist guerrillas, using drug revenues to finance their war.

Hundreds of Phipocians gathered at the consulate gate to protest what they considered the outrageous American action against their economy. The two uniformed Marines were ordered not to engage the rioters unless attacked.

The Marines retreated to a barricade in front of the consulate's thick wooden doors, automatic weapons and stun grenades at the ready. The remainder of the staff gathered on the second floor of the building. From the large conference room that opened out onto a porch, they watched the mob swell. Some of the protesters waved banners saying "Americans Go Home." Others threw stones that bounced off the heavy metal grates that protected the downstairs windows. The Phipoc police seemed content to stand at the margin of the crowd offering neither comfort nor resistance.

An acrobatic young Phipocian scaled the iron fence that separated the consulate grounds from the street. He scampered across the grassy area and began to climb up the side of the building. Using jutting bricks as hand-holds, he ascended to the base of the porch and swung himself onto the flagpole that held the United States flag. His back was just feet away from the room where the frightened consulate staff had gathered.

Smyth pushed his way to the front of the group, his right hand holding a .45 automatic. If the young man attempted to enter, Smyth would shoot him. But the climber did not enter. Instead, he pulled out a knife and began slashing at the cords that bound the flag to the pole. Smyth instantly holstered his weapon, raced to the porch and shimmied out onto the flagpole.

The young man glanced back, drove his knife deeply into Smyth's right leg, then returned to slashing the flag's bindings. Undaunted by the wound, Smyth tightened his grip on the precariously bending flagpole and slammed his right shoe hard into the young man's backside. The kick sent the protester flying off the end of the pole. For a moment, the young man clung to a corner of the flag.

Smyth pulled out his .45 and smashed its butt against the young man's fingers. The young Phipocian screamed, let go of the flag and fell to the grassy lawn. He lay still for a moment. The mob was suddenly silent, poised to rush the building. But then the young man moved and slowly rose to his feet. Smyth didn't wait for what might come next. Before anyone could react, he crawled back onto the porch and into the relative safety of the conference room.

"Well done," the counsel general said, slapping Smyth on the shoulder. "We caught it all on camera." The public affairs officer raised his camera in triumph. Two weeks later, *Time* magazine's cover featured a color photo of the event with the headline "Protester Gets the Boot, Not the Flag." Smyth's kick was the rare bright spot in the darkening story of America's defeat in Vietnam.

Smyth won a promotion, followed by prime postings to Moscow, Paris and Cairo. It was in the Egyptian capital that his beloved wife had been killed in a terrorist bombing targeting the American Embassy. Broken hearted, he returned to action, leading numerous anti-terrorist operations. He ultimately retired to their dream home in Parrot's Caw. There, he cultivated his garden, played golf and helped create The Martini Club.

9
Martini Time

A YEAR HAD passed since Smyth hosted the initial meeting of The Martini Club. It was his turn again, and he wanted to make the meeting memorable. As the group's only retired CIA operative, he decided to give a bad imitation of James Bond. He donned a dress shirt, topped by a brilliant red bow tie, a suave black dinner jacket and tartan shorts. "I love to show off my legs," he said as he greeted the members.

Smyth's legs were large and hairy, and undoubtedly would have been a turn off to his male guests, except for the ragged scar that ran down much of the length of his right calf.

"Hooker got ya?" quipped Mike Rose, a retired brothel owner from Nevada. "Happens to guys who don't pay up for services rendered."

"Watch your tongue," Smyth growled back in mock anger, "while you still have one." He smiled a playful, wicked smile.

The other members tacitly decided the less said about Smyth's leg the better and moved swiftly to the shakers filled with silvery martinis. Since, by custom, the host must pour the opening round, the members had to settle momentarily for hors d'oeuvres. The assortment included steaming hot Swedish meatballs skewered with tiny plastic daggers and slivers of cheese atop crackers. Typically, the hosting member's wife prepared the hors d'oeuvres then discreetly disappeared. Tonight, Smyth was the sole host.

"I got the meatballs from the Gourmet Foods Market in the mall," he said. "Who needs a wife if you've got a gourmet food store?" Nobody answered, but they sensed a momentary tone of grief in his voice.

Even at seventy, Smyth looked like a stereotypical CIA field operative. He was just under six feet with a burley, hard build, brush-cut graying hair over a ruggedly chiseled face. He still moved with the agility of an athlete. His intelligent steel gray eyes could be both menacing and friendly. He was not a man you would want to meet in a dark alley. His stories could be dark or funny, but were always fascinating. After telling a tale, he would add, "Remember, we are old men gathered together for the sole purpose of getting drunk while telling lies to one another." He would then roar with laughter, and begin another story.

"There was the time the company had to terminate an asset that had been turned. Our Israeli friends offered to liquidate him with a poison-tipped umbrella. The Brits recommended the Russian technique—a radioactive cocktail delivered at lunch. The blame, of course, would fall to the Russians. We, at the Company, are simple folk, so we just ran him over with a laundry truck—a nice, straightforward accident."

"The booze!" roared Rose, whose gravelly voice might have intimidated pimps, whores and dissatisfied tourists but not Smyth, who smiled his deadly smile and continued.

"I have made these martinis with gins created for higher, more sensitive pallets than those assembled here…oh ye' whose taste buds rival those of mountain gorillas. I pity your poor state and hope to improve your lot." He started to pour, then stopped yet again—a collective groan rose from his guests. "This is too poignant a moment to let pass without some ceremonial approbation," Smyth pontificated. "Rabbi Ginsberg, don't you Jews have a prayer before imbibing? Kindly do us the honor."

Nathan Ginsberg shrugged. Since retiring, the Reform rabbi had dedicated himself to destroying any image of Jewish males as teetotalers. Though he had come to drinking rather late in life, he found his conversion from ceremonial wine and occasional schnapps to martinis a swift and enlightening journey.

His alcoholic ride followed rapidly after the death of his wife Beth, who had shared his life for thirty-four years. She fought an all too brief battle against cancer. He still had three adult children whose busy lives left little room for a father who they saw as supremely and conveniently independent. He had sought solace first in prayer, then in good works, then in lonely drinking. He finally found it in the congeniality of The Martini Club. The members shared not only his love for the beneficent beverage, but for the accompanying intellectual discussions of matters both grave and frivolous. He saw the gathering—with its banter, laughter, raised voices and even shouting—as the natural progression from the minyan, the traditional Jewish gathering for communal ritual.

"Say the damn prayer," Smyth ordered, "before we all die of thirst."

The rabbi nodded. "Baruch atah Adonai, Eloheinu melech ha-olam, bore p'ri hagafen," he proclaimed in Hebrew. He repeated the prayer in English. "We praise you Eternal God, King of the Universe who created the fruit of the vine and the grain that gives forth booze. That's not an exact translation, but Amen. Let's drink."

Smyth savored his beverage, holding it up to the light streaming in from a nearby window. "I am offering you two of the world's finest gins gentlemen," he began. "Todd Morgan's Gin is a product of Girvan, Scotland. You will note that it is crystal clear, yet with a tinge of oily smoothness at the surface. After straining through various botanicals, the alcohol was given just the essence of cucumber and rose petal—a delight in aroma as well as taste. Delicious, but perhaps not for all. Let us turn our attention to its brave comrade, Iceland Cold Gin. It restores the dominance of juniper with a hint of orange and lemon peel, coriander, licorice, cinnamon, cassia, nutmeg, angelica and orris root, known not only for its aroma but also for its aphrodisiac qualities. The piece de resistance is its water content. The glacial water that dilutes this spirit to its consumable level comes from Iceland, where you find the purest, softest water on earth. I recommend you taste both brands. You will conclude there is no best between them, only a passage from one beautiful venue to another."

The club members brought their martini glasses to their lips and sipped. The first sip was always the most telling—the receptors of the tongue and nose not yet numbed by the icy anesthetic, the eyes clear, the brain alert in anticipation. Half the group had received the Todd Morgan; half the Iceland Cold. All concluded that they had tasted ambrosia. A few more sips and they would be as wise and witty as the gods.

10
A Not So Modest Proposal

Brody Brady nursed his drink with more than typical care—a swirl, a sniff, a savor on the palette, but only a small swallow. He was about to convince his friends to invest in a deal that would make them all rich—maybe, possibly, probably. *Okay,* he thought. *It's a crapshoot, but so what! They would be back in the game again, wheeling and dealing, thinking through their next move. It was the action that gave life its excitement, and this would put them squarely back in the action.*

Though he'd always craved to be part of the action, his "aha" moment came years ago while dining one evening with a successful garage builder. T. Benson Moore had hired Brady as his public relations man during his company's expansion into a number of other commercial ventures. Brady remembered sitting with Moore at a table in one of Long Island's fancier restaurants when three members of the town's board of trustees walked in. Moore waved them over and asked them to sit. After the usual small talk, Moore turned to Brady. "Go to the bar and get yourself a drink on my tab." Moore wanted no witnesses to the rest of the conversation.

Brady sat at the bar and drank. A half hour later, Moore joined him. "We had a nice talk," he laughed. "We all saw eye to eye in the end."

"Talk, schmalk," Brady countered. "You were bribing those guys. I want you to know I don't cotton to bribery. Plus, you've got more money than God. Why in hell do you have to pay off these guys to get approval for a motel and gas station rezoning that you don't need?"

Moore patted Brady's back. He was almost as tall as Brady, and considerably wider. Moore often referred to himself as portly; others called him fat, but never to his face. Wealth brought a certain deference. "It's not about the money. It's all about me being in the game, Brody boy. Besides, I didn't offer them bribes. I simply made generous donations to their campaign funds. It's the American way...and above all else, I am a patriot."

Brady long ago had learned that there were ethics and situational ethics. While he found bribery unethical, he could justify campaign contributions to elected officials who agreed with the giver's convictions—in this case that a new motel and gas station would be good for the community.

Brady's mind circled back to the present. *In all good conscience, I can't let these vastly talented men walk away from the game while there are still moves to be made. They are too valuable to spend their remaining years golfing, playing cards, taking endless pictures of their grandchildren and getting drunk with boon companions. Bringing them back in the game is simply the right thing to do.*

As the glow in his cheeks replaced the paleness of sobriety, Brady announced, "I am engaged in a business deal of monumental proportions. Out of the goodness of my heart, I am going to share it with you."

"Hold on to your wallets," laughed Sam Grieger.

"Silly boy," Brady responded. "I bring nothing but opportunity. Have you ever heard of switchgrass?"

"That's the stuff they talk about replacing gasoline," Grieger replied. "I've got some growing behind my condo. You can harvest it and stuff it in your gas tank, right?"

Grieger had spent thirty years of his life chasing scammers, con men, mobsters and occasionally murderers. He'd heard it all, and seen a lot of it—the slick bankers making mega deals with officials whose municipalities placed hundreds of millions of dollars in public money in their banks. "Where we put public funds is discretionary," they'd say. "Perfectly legal."

At the less sophisticated end of the business spectrum was Big Benny Schline. Grieger had covered a murder where Big Benny was accused of beating to death a union organizer with a claw hammer. Reportedly, Big Benny was in the employ of Bernardo Gui, a mob boss who earned a living breaking unions. The one witness against Big Benny lost his memory while on the stand. The jury acquitted. "You can quote me as saying, I am a nice guy who don't do such things of which I was accused," Big Benny told reporters on the courthouse steps. A week later he was indicted for extortion.

Shortly after the indictment, Grieger's wife Sheila got a call from Big Benny. "If Sam wants a great story, he should call 555-7113, ask for Gloria and follow instructions."

Sheila relayed the message to her husband word for word. "He was nice and polite and soft spoken, not like some of those politicians who call here."

"Big Benny Schline is a professional hit man," Grieger replied without trying to sound condescending. "Being nice and polite and soft spoken is the way hit men do business." He wanted Sheila to understand the difference between professional killers and politicians. "Hit men don't want to stand out because of the nature of their work." The possibility of a big story, however, could not be ignored.

Sam dialed the phone as instructed and asked for Gloria, who answered with a deep, base voice. "Drive to the Seagram Circle dead end by the beach, then park. You got thirty minutes." Click. That was it.

"I'll be home late, Sheila. Don't wait up." She had already put dinner away, and handed him a thermos of coffee as he left. He had an understanding wife.

As he drove to Seagram Circle, Grieger reviewed his theory about dealing with the Big Bennies and Bernardo Guis of this world. *If you don't do business with them, don't borrow money from them and don't marry their daughters, they have no reason to kill you or break your legs. They are essentially businessmen. There is no profit in killing reporters. Well, marrying their daughters might change the equation.*

It took Grieger just under thirty minutes to drive to Seagram Circle. It was one of those cul-de-sacs that ended in marshy woods. No houses, no cars parked for the night. He turned off his engine. And he waited.

Moments later an unshaven man appeared at the driver's side window. "Get into the car parked behind you."

"You sound a lot like Gloria," Grieger said as he exited his vehicle.

"I am Gloria," the man replied.

Grieger followed instructions and got into the front passenger seat. Gloria got in behind him and blindfolded him. Grieger questioned whether his theory about no profit in killing reporters was actually valid.

They drove for about a half hour.

"Get out," Gloria said.

Grieger found the door handle, opened the door and staggered to his feet. He started to remove his blindfold when a hairy hand stopped him. "I'll tell you when," Gloria said in his no nonsense voice.

He was guided up a flight of outside stairs. He heard a door open. "Take the blindfold off when you get inside, and turn left. Don't trip," Gloria advised. "I wouldn't want to see you get hurt."

Grieger did as he was told. When he took off his blindfold, he caught a glimpse of a woman and a child watching a cartoon on television in a living room. They ignored his entry. Grieger was steered down a flight of stairs into a partially finished basement of what appeared to be a private home. The basement door closed behind him.

The room was large, but the windows were small—too small to crawl through. The basement was brightly lit by four sets of fluorescent bulbs, which gave a shiny finish to the cheap cream-colored linoleum floor. The walls were a rough cinderblock. The only furniture was a table and two chairs placed roughly in the center of the room. Grieger wondered if he could pull a leg off one of the chairs if he had to defend himself.

The basement door opened and Big Benny Schline started down the stairs. He was not a tall man, maybe five foot ten. He had a hard build. He was wearing a white T-shirt, the sleeves stretched tight by his bulging biceps. Thick blue veins guided the muscles of his arms. Grieger noticed a whiskey bottle in Big Benny's right hand. *Is he going to beat me to death with a cheap bottle of booze?*

As Big Benny reached the last step, he smiled and pulled two shot glasses out of his pocket. In the soft voice that so captivated Sheila Grieger earlier in the day, he said, "Sammy, let's drink some shots while I give you the biggest story of your life. In a nutshell, my business partner is Chief Assistant District Attorney Bryon Hatfield, the same guy who is prosecuting me for extortion. The son-of-a-bitch just decided he didn't want to split our profits. He wants to have it all." Between shots, Big Benny gave the names of individuals and dummy corporations involved in illegal land grabs, insurance fraud and case tampering. It was a big story indeed.

I was right, Grieger thought as Gloria drove him back to his car blindfolded. *There is no profit in killing a reporter when you can use him to screw somebody else.*

11
Once Upon a Time

They had been drinking and nibbling at meatballs, cold shrimp, cheese and other delicacies for almost an hour before Brody Brady made his pitch.

Already on his second martini, Grieger found it easy to see a parallel between Big Bennie's friend Gloria and Brody Brady. One had taken him to what could have been a dangerous place; the other was about to do so. This time Grieger knew he shouldn't go along for the ride. Nevertheless, he felt a twinge of excitement for the first time in a long time. "Okay, let's hear the full pitch," he snapped at Brady.

Brady knew cynicism or at least a healthy skepticism was part of the journalist's code, but he sensed Grieger and the others could be tempted into one more adventure. They were all getting bored with the slow pace of retired life.

Brady turned to Smyth. "Bartender, kindly refill the gentlemen's glasses and be sure to include yourself. I am about to tell you a wonderful tale that is rife with opportunity for us all." Smyth, curious, quickly complied.

Brady went on to educate his friends about switch-grass and how it would make all of them millions. He began by noting that back in the early 2000s former President George W. Bush had spotlighted the grass as part of America's drive to attain clean energy independence. "This humble, virtually inedible, almost useless weed not only will reduce the country's tragic dependence on foreign oil by producing millions of gallons of ethanol, but it will put an end to the country's practice of using corn as its major ethanol source."

After pausing for dramatic effect, Brady offered his view of the dire situation and how The Martini Club could help save the stars and stripes—in fact, the world—from disaster. "Corn should be used to feed the hungry. The marquee on this nation's multiplex of reusable energy has switchgrass writ large. Now is the time. Stuarton is the place. We can be a part of this revolution." Brady spread his arms wide, bowed and waited for a round of applause. Instead, he heard nothing.

"He wants money from us...lots of money," intoned Rabbi Ginsberg. "He wants my pension. Jesus threw people like him out of the temple for stuff like this. And right now Brody boy you are standing at the temple door."

"You do me a cruel injustice," Brady countered. "I too believe that wherever The Martini Club meets is holy ground, a place where men reveal their souls, their inner thoughts. I would never desecrate such hallowed ground. For a man of the cloth to accuse me of being a swindler in so sacred a place cuts me deeply. It is blasphemy, but I forgive you. I have a warm if not always generous heart, especially for clergy. They try so hard and do so little."

"You'll have to wait for Yom Kippur for me to forgive you," the rabbi shot back. "Or maybe for the cow to jump over the moon...whichever comes later."

They drank and ate without speaking for a time. Jay Corrigan, the pilot, broke the silence. "If you tied the cow's ass to a Saturn rocket, you should be able to blast it over the moon. But the cow would need a breathing apparatus, presuming you want the cow to come back alive. When do you think NASA would approve blasting a cow over the moon?" he asked his comrades.

"Not sure," Smyth replied, "but would blasting the cow over the moon technically be the same as the cow jumping over the moon?'"

"Before Brady says another word," Grieger interrupted, "I think he should explain his role in the recent riot at the clubhouse. And speaking of ass, he hired a hooker for the event."

"She wasn't a hooker, and I didn't hire her," Brady shot back. "I simply made some suggestions to our somewhat unimaginative young property manager, Chris Bideau."

"I understand you also made a profit," the retired reporter went on. "And not so long ago, there was another multi-million-dollar deal you urged us to invest in. It turned out to be a scam. That time we were going to help build a world trade center just outside Stuarton. We were lucky the thing went belly up before we got involved. So why should we trust you now?"

"We were so close, so close!" Brady sighed.

The center had been the brainchild of a group from Stuarton that hired Brady to sell Chinese businessmen on the idea of investing in a New Universal Trade Center on the outskirts of the city. The Chinese were to invest ten million dollars and move part of their business operations to Stuarton. The rest of the money for the hundred million dollar project was to be raised locally by selling shares in the newly formed New Universal Trade Center Corporation, also known by its acronym NUTCC.

During his time in Washington, Brady had made a connection with the Chinese government's unofficial lobbying group, known as the Chinese-American Cooperative Capitalist Association. Brady convinced the Chinese to pledge more than a million dollars before the project collapsed. A local bank and a large number of Stuarton residents also invested. Ultimately, NUTCC failed to come up with enough hard cash to close on the site for the center, which would have included a ten-story, all-glass structure.

As the project began falling apart, NUTCC's chairman of the board, president, treasurer and secretary voted themselves hundred-thousand-dollar bonuses. The bank and a large number of Stuarton residents were now suing the four corporate officers, who also faced fraud indictments.

The Martini Club members remembered how close they'd come to investing after Brady pitched them. "Get in while there is a ton of money to be made," he had counseled. "Your stock will be worth a fortune when the company goes public." Fortunately, the group had moved too slowly on Brady's advice.

"I was fooled along with the rest of you," Brady protested. "I suffered and am suffering. My credibility with the Chinese is gone. And the federal government may want me to testify whether NUTCC was a fraud from the beginning. But my new deal is not the same. I have vetted the man behind it, and he is gold, solid gold, very deep pockets."

Rabbi Ginsberg, having finished testing both gins, announced, "Brody you are a good man to drink with and to be friends with, but a dangerous man to invest with. I once gave a wonderful sermon on drinking and the dangerous people you meet that way. I wish I'd known you back then. I could have made an even better sermon. You would have added another dimension."

Grieger had been weighing his position in this debate. He and Sheila got along well on their pensions, 401ks and Social Security. She had worked in finance and done extremely well. He had worked for a newspaper that had demonstrated unusual generosity for that industry. However, that didn't mean they had extra money to throw around. On the other hand, Brady's schemes added a dash of excitement that Grieger had been missing since he'd retired as a reporter and editor.

"Rabbi, you least of all, should rush to judgment," he said. "Let's hear how Brody is going to make us all millions. As a journalist for nearly forty years, I chronicled the doings of scam artists, con men, politicians and mob guys. Brody is not of that mold. He's an American authentic, the ultimate entrepreneur and, the ultimate risk taker. I say we listen to his full pitch. It may be all bullshit, or rather cow shit, from over the moon, but I believe we need more information before we can decide whether Brody is dropping shit or golden eggs. Expound further, brother Brody. You haven't told us how switchgrass will make us a dime."

Brady's slender frame stretched over his rounded back, giving him the appearance of a large question mark. His thick white hair and handsome, lined face, however, still signaled a man of depth and gravitas. The base registers of his voice resonated. He was a man who demanded attention.

As he prepared to address the group, he stood straight up. At his true six-foot-two- inches, Brady was actually a somewhat imposing figure. The members of The Martini Club had learned long ago to be wary of this delightful and convincing salesman, but the more they drank, the more vulnerable they became to his charms.

After a theatrical pause, Brady began. "I am glad there still remains some intelligent curiosity among you ancients…some who, though long in tooth and hairy in nose, remain wise in the ways of opportunity. *Carpe Diem*, gentlemen. It is time to seize the day!"

12
The Stuarton Business Club

GRIEGER LOOKED ACROSS the room and observed Smyth's collection of guns and daggers poised against the wall, as if ready for some imminent attack. "Hold on, Brady. Where did you come up with this wacky deal?"

"Well," Brady began, "it all started at The Stuarton Business Club..."

An organization ostensibly set up to do good deeds for the city, The Stuarton Business Club held charity balls and other fundraising events such as bridge runs, cake sales and so-called "shmushing" events in which members—dressed as clowns and locked in stocks—let children throw pies and giant marshmallows at them. A direct hit was a "shmush." Those who got "shmushed" would have to contribute fifty bucks to a local charity. The club's primary purpose, though, was to serve as a networking organization for its members—bankers, lawyers, businessmen and public officials. It held monthly luncheons at which members could exchange views, listen to speakers and, of course, arrange deals. It was at such a luncheon that Brady met the New Universal Trade Center boys.

"The business club is Stuarton's development hub," Brady went on. "A single membership costs five-thousand dollars a year, a steep sum for such a modest city, but it keeps the riffraff out and offsets the expense of providing free memberships for public officials."

Lunch at The Stuarton Business Club was typically covered as well, excluding hard liquor, for which thirsty members paid out of pocket. The members took turns as speakers, though on occasion they would bring in an outsider with special knowledge of business or the economy. A local professor of finance was a business club favorite for many years, repeatedly making appearances to expound on the ups and downs of the stock market.

Several of the business club's members were so taken with the professor's knowledge that they gave him money to invest for them. In return, he charged a substantial consulting fee. The professor's eccentricity—and thus presumed wisdom—was marked by a multicolored robe, which he wore for these speaking engagements. The robe reached down to the professor's shoes, covered his substantial paunch, and had a luminance that dazzled the minds of business club members. The robe did, however, cause a problem when the professor used the urinal. Members preferred not to share the men's room with him. The professor was later convicted of fraud after his investors learned he used their money to buy obscure, nearly worthless works of art.

"Are you suggesting we invest with the dashiki dressing economics professor, if we can find his prison?" asked Smyth sarcastically.

"No, no, no," Brady responded.

"So get to the point," Smyth demanded.

"First you chastise me. Then you want me to rush the story along. You are a difficult bunch of drunks. I'd hate to think of you sober," Brady groaned, resigned to the barbs that regularly flew among Martini Club members. But he knew he had their attention. He paused, once again straightened to his full height, and the pitchman began his tale.

13
Flashback

Brady was bored by The Stuarton Business Club's current speaker, an expert on new technologies. He quietly left his table at the luncheon and moved to the bar.

"A child-sized gin martini, bartender."

"I'll have the same as that gentleman," said a man who suddenly appeared next to him.

"Bad heart?"

"Bad something. Doctor tells me to take it easy on the booze. My name is Bideau, Rufus Bideau." He extended his hand to Brady.

"Hi, I'm Brody Brady. Aren't you the developer of Parrot's Caw?"

"I am. President and sole stockholder of RB&S—Rufus Bideau and Sons. My boys work for me. And you are the man who hooked my Chris up with the stripper for the opening of the Parrot's Caw condominium section. Made for quite a show." Bideau did not attempt to hide the sarcasm in his deep voice.

For a moment, Brady expected the encounter to turn unpleasant. "A simple misunderstanding."

Bideau smiled a cold smile. "Of course. Just a misunderstanding. Nobody hurt except for that pimp that my son had to restrain. But let's move on. I hear you almost made a success of that New Universal Trade Center despite the scammers. I was going to put a few dollars into that myself before everything fell apart. I am a venture capitalist."

With that, the developer picked up his glass and suggested they move to one of the little raised tables outside the dining room. Brady quickly rose and led the way. *This Bideau clearly is a numbers man—profit and loss are all that matter.*

They sat and sipped their martinis, both enjoying the consuming warmth. "Brady, if you are the man I think you are, I have a proposition for you. First, however, I must give you a bit of education."

In great detail, Bideau recounted the recent history of switchgrass, spotlighting its potential as both a fuel and an asset to the environment. He concluded with an appeal to Brady's heart and wallet.

"The switchgrass movement's major difficulty is the corn lobby, which has convinced Congress to legislate huge subsidies for farmers who produce corn for conversion to ethanol. Now every damn fool in the world knows that corn is a food and should be produced to feed people and the animals that feed people. Reducing the amount of corn available for food and forage means scarcity. This, in turn, means the price of food and just about everything else goes up. Think about the neediest among us slavering for cheap, hot buttered corn on the cob. It won't be available to them anymore. Too expensive. Or how about the poor motorists, like you and me, when gasoline climbs back to four dollars a gallon or more? Brady, have you ever heard of Verde Bioenergy?"

"No."

"It's part of a huge international Spanish firm," Bideau said. "Its latest financial report shows Verde made more than one billion Euros in profit last year. That's more than a billion U.S. dollars. Being big and international with lobbyists of its own, Verde was able to do what you and I couldn't do. It convinced the U.S. government to guarantee one hundred and thirty-two million dollars for a construction loan to build the company's first-of-a-kind commercial-scale bio-refinery. Unlike a fossil-fuel refinery, a bio-refinery is effectively a mechanical cow. It munches on switchgrass, slides the mash down its gullet into one of its stomachs, turns it into a thick mush and finally ferments and distills it into ethanol."

Bideau took another sip of his martini and waited for Brady to do the same. "Do you know where that plant is going to be built?" Bideau asked rhetorically. Then, proceeded to answer his own question. "Not here where there's enough switchgrass to build forty bio-refineries. No. It's being built in the little nothing of a town of Victorton, Iowa—a small, rural community with fewer than four-thousand residents. It's out in the middle of nowhere."

"What does this all mean to me or Stuarton?"

"Perhaps a hundred-million-dollar switchgrass bio-refinery plant, if Verde decides to come to Stuarton. The machinery has begun to turn. Money has changed hands. Permits are being obtained or assured. All on the quiet, of course. Only a handful of people know."

"It doesn't seem any of these big players would need *my* money."

"True. But I know something they don't, and sharp businessmen like us can turn that information into a cornucopia of cash. All it would take is a quick one-million-dollar investment to make tens of millions of dollars or more—not a bad return."

"A one-million-dollar investment in what?"

"There is a five-hundred-acre farm for sale right near the proposed Stuarton plant. The owner is dying and thinks his land isn't worth much, but he wants to leave his kin some cash. If we move fast, we can buy the farm and start supplying that refinery with switchgrass for the rest of its days. The farmer wants a million and a half, but I'm sure I can talk him down to a million. You can bet his price would double, if he heard about the plant, which is supposed to come online in about eighteen months to two years."

"Where's this farm located?"

"That's my little secret, until we have a signed deal and the million."

"I don't have one million dollars to invest Mr. Bideau, but I will put the proposition to my associates."

With that, Bideau and Brady left their empty martini glasses and headed back to the luncheon, where the expert on new technologies droned on.

14
Skepticism

THE MARTINI CLUB members stared at their hors d'oeuvres and sipped their drinks quietly in contemplation. Finally, David Neville, a lawyer and accountant, broke the mood. "Brody, your track record is not—and I emphasize the word NOT—good. In fact, it stinks. And now you want us to come up with one million dollars to buy a farm that grows a grass that nobody wants, but might want someday? I think the only grass worth thinking about is the stuff you must have been smoking before you entered this room."

Mike Rose swallowed the remaining liquid in his glass, "Hold on. You bean counters have no imagination, no foresight. Maybe, just maybe, Brady is onto something this time. It kind of reminds me of the time I started bringing in gay prostitutes when everybody was saying it was a bad mix with straights, being that they were my main clientele. Turned out, the straights loved it. Some of them actually experimented with switch-hitting. It opened up more options, so to speak." Rose and a few others chuckled at the double meaning.

"The Martini Club is an institution for drinking and arguing," Neville shot back. "It is not your local investment club or a whorehouse. Nobody in his right mind drinks this many martinis and starts making investment decisions. Brady brings us this cockamamie tale of meeting some insider who out of the blue offers him the equivalent of the Brooklyn Bridge, and all he needs in return is for ten drunk dummies to cough up a hundred thousand apiece. I don't think so. Drunk or sober, it's a lousy idea."

Rose lowered his glass and opened his jacket, revealing his holstered SigSauer Pro 9mm pistol. "Are you calling me a drunk dummy?" he growled in mock anger.

Smyth shot Rose his killer look. Rose winced as if struck by a pellet and closed his jacket. "I wasn't going to shoot him," he said. "Hey, look, I'm either a drunk or a dummy, but not both. That crosses the line."

"I know," Smyth replied. "But flashing that thing is not friendly, and The Martini Club has standards of friendliness. Verbal attacks and sarcasm are permitted. Anything beyond that is not. Sort of a sticks and stones policy."

"He wouldn't have shot me," Neville added with a lack of certainty in his voice.

"Maybe," Smyth answered. "But as host I want to be sure we maintain a certain decorum. You see, decorum was very important at the Company, and I intend to maintain that tradition within The Martini Club."

"You mean no blood stains on the carpets?" Rose asked with a laugh. "As a Libertarian, I believe in limiting rules, regulations and restrictions. One of the beautiful things about The Martini Club is that it has none. I also have every right to bear arms anywhere under the Second Amendment, and that includes here."

Smyth smiled his assassin smile, and refilled Rose's martini glass.

Brady rose to his full height again, and continued his pitch. "Now that we have explored some of the issues, let me say that I anticipated your skepticism, as did Mr. Bideau. It's natural for a deal this size. I will have one of his representatives available to answer your questions at my place tomorrow afternoon. I will serve martinis to those who wish to imbibe—or you can just listen and question soberly."

All the members agreed, except for Ginsberg. "Tomorrow is Wednesday. I can't make it."

"Thursday then," Brady countered.

"Fine. I'm in," the rabbi replied. So were the rest.

15
Ginsberg Goes Shopping

Wednesdays had become a ritual for Nathan Ginsberg. They were senior discount days at the Best Food Buys supermarket. While he detested shopping, he recognized that it was an essential function of daily living. Ten percent off wasn't bad either.

Routines, such as his Wednesday shopping trips, had become increasingly important in his life. At home there were only memories of his wife Beth, and the increasing desire for alcohol. Setting small daily outside goals kept him from becoming an alcoholic. Ginsberg knew he did not want to spend his days sitting on a couch, wrapped in a bathrobe, watching old movies and sipping whiskey.

This Wednesday was no different. He entered Best Food Buys and secured a cart. His first stop was the deli department, where he prepared to pick up his usual choices—a quarter pound of roast beef, not too rare, a quarter pound of low-sodium turkey breast, and a quarter pound of his favorite horseradish cheddar cheese.

"Want to try something different today?" asked Frankie from behind the giant display case. "We have some delicious London Port roast beef that will put some spice in your life."

"My stomach says yes, but my heartburn says no," Ginsberg responded with a smile. He had gotten to know Frankie quite well over time, and liked him. Frankie brought a rare enthusiasm to an occupation that involved eight hours a day of slicing meat and cheese for just over the minimum wage.

"Maybe next time," Frankie responded. "You'll see I'm right about the London Port. It will change your life."

"My life has been changed enough," the rabbi responded with a hint of sadness. The memory of shopping with Beth flashed through his mind. "Maybe next time," he added, not wanting to disappoint Frankie.

Ginsberg rolled his shopping cart mechanically to his next stop—fruits and vegetables. He always picked up three bananas, more and they would go bad before he could eat them. Then came the strawberries, raspberries and blackberries, always in that order. He had become aware that when he departed from his routine, he frequently forgot an item. He now worked carefully from a list he prepared at home.

It was time to select the vegetables. He picked up two tomatoes, a small head of lettuce and two pounds of potatoes. He contemplated getting some string beans. They weren't on his list, but he hadn't had them for a while. And the list did not prohibit him from adding items. He paused, then seized a plastic bag from the rack near the vegetable scale and headed quickly toward the beans.

A woman, half bent over, was snapping beans to test their freshness. Ginsberg, waiting behind her, realized he was admiring her ass, which was nicely outlined by her tight slacks. He stepped closer, and had to suppress a desire to reach out and touch it. Suddenly, she stood up and turned directly into him, spilling some of her hand-selected beans on him and the floor.

"So sorry," Ginsberg said, embarrassed. He knelt and began picking them up. "No point crying over spilled beans," he croaked, trying to make a joke.

She smiled. "Don't bother. I can get some more." She turned back to the mass of string beans.

"May I ask a favor?" Ginsberg blurted out.

"What?" the woman replied, again offering a smile.

"Could you help me pick out about a quarter pound of those beans. The last time I picked beans, I found half of them were rotten. I know so little about shopping that I thought string beans were actually strung together." She laughed and stared, evaluating him for the first time—mid-sixties, good looking, nice build, and a wedding ring on his left hand.

He noticed her glancing at his ring. He also was struck by her deep green eyes and her unadorned left ring finger.

"I'm sorry. I shouldn't have asked," he said contritely. "Ever since my wife died, I have had to do my own food shopping. I must admit I find it confusing."

She looked at him more thoughtfully. "Let's do this together. First, if you are selecting string beans, look them over for mold or spots. Next, snap one or two and taste one. The snap should be sharp, and the taste should be, well, tasty." They both smiled.

Ginsberg watched dutifully as the woman demonstrated and filled his plastic bag with almost precisely a quarter pound of beans. Together they toured the market's twenty-three aisles, selecting various items for their carts. He saw that she occasionally checked a list of her own, and kept to it more stringently than he did. When they reached the paper products section, she turned to Ginsberg and said, "My name is Mary. What's yours?"

"Nathan, Nathan Ginsberg." He felt a bit giddy. "After we check out, would you allow me to buy you a cup of coffee?"

She studied him. He had a sweetness and naiveté about him. "Sure. There's a food court at the end of the market area. Let's check out and push our carts there." She was not ready to have him walk her to her car.

They sat at a high, round table that gave them a wide view of the multitude of shoppers passing through on their way to the mall's far end, where a Sears sat as the anchor store. They people watched and quietly sipped their coffee.

"If you are trying to pick me up, you are going to have to tell me more about your wife and why you still wear your wedding ring."

He slowly spun the ring on the third finger of his left hand. "My wife died of cancer almost two years ago. Our wedding ring is just part of me, like she was."

"I'm so sorry about your wife. I shouldn't have asked."

"It's okay. It's a good question. As for your other question—about whether I am trying to pick you up—well, I guess maybe yes. I've never done that before, so I don't really know for sure. I do know I would like to make your acquaintance—unless you are attached."

"I am not attached."

They continued sipping coffee, looking at each other, neither knowing quite what to say next. Ginsberg's mind raced. *Was two years an appropriate period for his mourning to be over?* Until now, he had been obsessed with the past. Beth had been his lover, the mother of his children, his rebbitzen. She had made him feel warm and loved. She had critiqued his sermons. She had endured his paltry pay when he started out with a tiny congregation in Oklahoma. She had worked at a jewelry store to make ends meet. But she had been gone now for two years, and he was sixty-five years old, healthy, retired and very lonely.

Mary broke the silence. "So let's start again. This time, total honesty. My name is Mary Latham. I am fifty years old and divorced from a man who turned from kind and understanding to cruel and violent. After ten years together, something in him changed, and in the process, he lost me."

"I am so sorry," Ginsberg responded. "Perhaps it would be better to go back to talking about string beans."

"I have said too much," Mary sighed.

"You said total honesty, so here goes. I am sixty-five and have two beautiful adult children who are too busy to pay much attention to their old man, so I try to keep out of their way. I am also a retired Reform rabbi."

"A rabbi," Mary repeated with surprise. "I never met a rabbi before. I am a lapsed Christian. Are rabbis allowed to pick up women?"

"We can drink, smoke and romance women. The only thing we can't do is adultery. We try to abide by the six hundred and thirteen commandments God gave us, and that is one of them. Generally speaking, though, it is not good form for working rabbis to pick up women in supermarkets."

"So picking me up was bad form?" Mary teased.

"I'm retired, so luckily I don't have to explain my behavior to a temple board any more. They are always interested in appearances. Therefore, it was not bad form for me to seek out your acquaintance in a supermarket."

"Makes complete sense to me, except for trying to obey six hundred and thirteen rules. Could we be friends without me having to obey that many rules?"

"Of course! Nobody can obey all of them. We just give it a good college try."

"Understood," Mary smiled. "I also understand about having grown children who you rarely see."

They talked pleasantly for about twenty more minutes, finished their coffee, and faced the imminent transition awkwardly. "May I call you?" Ginsberg blurted.

Mary opened her purse, took out a pen and small piece of paper. "Sure." She wrote down her name and phone number. She pressed the paper into his hand. "Walk me to my car. You can help me with the bundles."

And so their love affair began.

16
Lovers

It started as a September song—bright like the leaves of autumn. Filled with the reds and greens and golds of passion. Hurried by the knowledge of the winter winds.

First, they had lunch daily at a small delicatessen that Ginsberg favored for its tangy pastrami sandwiches.

"A good pastrami sandwich begins with two slices of a good Jewish rye bread. Each slice must be slathered with spicy deli mustard. The pastrami slices must be thick, hot and ample," he told Mary.

"No mayonnaise?" she asked.

"Mayonnaise is definitely a no-no," he replied.

"Because it isn't kosher?"

"Because it makes a lousy sandwich."

They laughed. They took long walks around the city's artistic district. Mary introduced Ginsberg to the works of local artists like Carolyn Mae Laurie and Alfred Morris. She educated him on the use of light and color. He marveled at her knowledge.

"I was an art major until I realized I lacked the talent," she shared. "The experience left me with a great appreciation for those who have the eye and hand for art. I would say they have a gift from God."

"I agree. A great artist captures something the rest of us don't see, and makes it visible to all."

One day, after one of their longer walks, he invited her to his condo in Parrot's Caw. She went happily. The moment they entered the house, he closed the door and took her in his arms. They kissed deeply and longingly.

"I've wanted to do this for so long," he gasped.

"I wanted you to for so long," she whispered back.

They went down a long corridor to the master bedroom. Ginsberg stared at the bed he had shared with his wife for so many years.

"Let's go to the guest room," he said, regretting it the instant he uttered it. He felt her body tense.

"Am I just a guest?" she asked.

He looked at her silently for a long moment. Tears filled his eyes.

"No, you are not a guest. I just had the feeling I would be desecrating Beth's memory if we used this bed."

"I understand," Mary replied, "but Beth loved you. She would want you to go on with your life. She would want you to find happiness. I can only hope to love you the way she did." With that, she kissed him ever so gently on his lips. Her hands moved down and rubbed slowly against his bulging masculinity.

He undid the buttons of her blouse, then reached around and opened her bra, freeing her ample breasts. He cupped his hands around each of them. They moved together to the bed, each slowly removing the other's interfering clothing. Naked, they lay together. He entering her; she moving her soft hands slowly, then more hurriedly as their passions synchronized into one explosive moment. After, they slept the deep sleep of contented lovers.

17
Down on the Farm

Lucas Bideau was growing impatient. He had been waiting outside the Stuarton Plaza for more than an hour with nothing to do but drum his fingers on the steering wheel of the steel gray Mercedes Benz. Lucas hated the waiting part of being his daddy's chauffeur, bodyguard and enforcer. He had leafed through the latest copy of Playboy and closely examined the contents of two internet porn sites on his phone. There was nothing left to do except drum his thick fingers on the steering wheel.

Finally, Rufus Bideau appeared, his arm around the shoulder of a local banker. They stopped just outside the car and laughed at a joke Lucas could not hear through the vehicle's soundproof glass. Rufus slid into the rear seat. "First pick up my lawyer. Then, drive us out to old Caleb Lampkin's farm on the Post Road."

Lucas turned his head. "Why we visiting that old goat? He's near drunk himself dumb and blind, and hasn't worked that farm for years. There's nothing there but weeds."

"Precisely," Rufus replied. "That's why we soon will cultivate that farm into a one-million-dollar cash crop. Remember, 'as you sow, so shall ye reap.' Now drive."

Caleb Lampkin was in his usual state of drunkenness as he rocked slowly in an old wooden chair on his porch. The rocker tilted slightly to its left, a victim of Lampkin falling off on that side to avoid being bitten by a large, persistent spider that never left the old farmer's faltering gaze. Lampkin's formidable swats at the creature seemed to pass right through it and its growing web. Their constant battle was fought in his brain, the only outside casualty being the rocking chair.

Lampkin looked out over his acres of weed-filled land, cracked and hardened by lack of use. He thought back to the early years, when its yield of beets, beans, melons, tomatoes and corn brought in sufficient money to feed Martha and their kids. Then the drought came, followed by the voracious armyworms. The inch-long creatures came by the thousands, climbing up and down his plants, eating away his livelihood. They continued their destruction despite the farmer's relentless efforts to stop them. Finally, they morphed into ugly gray moths, leaving Lampkin and his farm as ugly and gray as their tiny, winged bodies. Martha passed away soon after. She died of an infection that led to a fatal heart attack. The kids moved in with their Aunt Sarah, who lived three hundred miles away.

Rufus Bideau's Mercedes stopped on the gravel driveway that led up to Lampkin's porch. As the farmer looked up, Rufus smiled his warm-cold smile. "Hello, Caleb. I have deal for you."

18
The Deal

Bideau eyed Lampkin from the top of his old brimmed and beaten hat to his unshaven face all the way down to his once brown boots, which were now nearly black, cracked and moldy. Lampkin leaned forward revealing an unwashed, sleeveless undershirt beneath faded coveralls. Rufus sniffed and brushed his nose hoping to limit the oncoming smell.

"You got that homemade whiskey smell to you, Lampkin. Stinks of feet. You sober enough to talk?"

"Sober enough to deal with the likes of you," Lampkin snapped, reaching for a rusty twelve-gauge shotgun hidden behind the open front door. "You're either a tax collector or a foreclosure server from the bank. You got ten seconds to skedaddle out of here before I fill you full of birdshot."

"I'm neither," Rufus Bideau replied, undeterred by the shotgun. "I'm here to offer you a deal."

Lampkin attempted to absorb the message. He lowered the shotgun slightly. "Deal?"

"Yes, a deal, Lampkin. I respect a man who works the soil. There is something deeply biblical about it. The first man God made, he called Adam, which means 'of the earth' in holy writ."

"God ain't touched this damn, drought-cracked earth in three years. So don't go comparing it to the Good Book."

"My apologies. You struck me as a Christian man."

"Used to be. Stopped when Martha died."

"I should have known. Yes, it comes back to me now. So what do you believe in?"

"Hell, damnation and the devil," Lampkin spit, finding his mouth thirsting for some whiskey.

"An interesting array of beliefs."

"I've already been damned and gone to hell. I'm just sitting here waiting for the devil to keep me company on my final trip."

Rufus raised his eyebrows. "So let's talk about that deal."

Lampkin put down the shotgun and waved Rufus into the house. Inside, he motioned Bideau to sit at what was once the dining room table. It was now covered with piles of unopened mail, mostly bills and notices. The electricity had been turned off more than a year ago, so had the water. Lampkin brought in the water he needed from a well in back of the farmhouse. Candles, firewood and paper supplied light and heat.

The farmer watched Bideau's eyes moving up and down the piles. "I'll use them to start my fireplace right after I get through tearing out pages from the Bible," he said. "These letters and the pages seem to burn just about the same, though the Bible pages give off a sort of sick-sweet smell. Must have better ink." He nodded toward what was left of his King James version.

"You might have a point there," Bideau responded. "May I move some of your mail back a bit to make room on the table? I would prefer we each sit on one of your chairs. As they sat, a small cloud of dust and mold rose. Outside, the spider scurried to repair its damaged web.

The straight-backed dining room chairs thus far had survived the ongoing decay and collapse of the other furnishings, and remained sturdy enough to hold the two men.

The floor creaked below them in a kind of forlorn protest. Lampkin wriggled his chair in response. "When we ate, Martha used to sit where you're sitting. She was a good cook. Made real tasty hominy grits cooked in milk and cheese, and her 'Hoppin' John' was hard to beat. But she ain't here no more. I just eat what I can shoot and what little I can make grow in the back field." Memories of more hospitable times kicked in. "I'd offer you something to eat or drink, but I got nothin'. That's my problem. I got nothin'."

Bideau pulled some papers from the inside of his jacket. "I think we can solve your problem, Farmer Lampkin. Simply put, here is the deal: I will pay off your mortgage, all the back taxes, your water and electric bills. In return, you will sell me your five hundred acres, including this good house, at two dollars an acre. I am prepared to pay you one thousand dollars in cash right now. As further compensation, I will allow you to live in your house free for ten years or until the day you die, whichever comes first. All I need is your signature on this deed transfer agreement."

Lampkin's eyes flickered—rational thoughts tried to fight their way passed the spider and back into his consciousness. "Why you doing this?" he managed. "Banks gonna come with a sheriff one day and toss me out. I'm gonna shoot the banker, and the sheriff's gonna shoot me. Then, I'll be on my way to the devil and real hell."

Bideau narrowed his gaze on Lampkin's face. He noted its black and white stubble, its deep wrinkles, the touch of spittle on the farmer's lips and the dim glow of a residual intelligence buried in the weathered farmer's blue-gray eyes. Bideau fished into the inner pocket of his jacket and withdrew a silver flask. He unscrewed the cap and placed the flask on the table. The aroma of pure bourbon escaped into the air. Lampkin's nostrils flared as he absorbed the scent.

"I have my reasons. Let's just say I see your farm as a well placed investment. You sign, and we can drink to our deal. As an added show of respect, I have formed a corporation to purchase the farm, and named it in your honor. It shall go into the Stuarton County records as the C. Lampkin Corporation."

"That's a real gentlemanly thing to do for me." Lampkin's bloodshot eyes narrowed. "You plan to dirty up my name as well as take my farm?"

"You mistake my intentions," Bideau answered with a wicked smile. "Let's just call it a memorial to you."

"I don't believe a word you say. But this farm's already taken my blood." Lampkin slumped slightly in his chair. "What's my choice anyway? Nobody's offered me a dime for this place. Don't really want to shoot the banker, though he deserves it. At least the farm will have my name, and I'll have a respectable home again—a place I can get my kids to come visit. Maybe they'll even come back and live here again."

"Precisely," Bideau replied. He reached into a pocket, this time withdrawing a gold and black pen. He offered it to the farmer. "Sign."

Something clicked in the farmer's foggy brain. "I want a copy of anything we sign, or you can just walk out the door."

"Of course." Reluctantly, Bideau drew out a duplicate document from his briefcase and placed it on the table beside the original. "Now, we can sign both."

As Lampkin scratched his name by the large, dark Xs, Bideau's son Lucas and another man entered the room. The man was small with scraggly gray hair. The farmer recognized him as a lawyer named Gideon Whipple. The other man was tall and muscular. "My son and my lawyer," Rufus Bideau whispered soothingly to Lampkin. "Here to witness our agreement. Just making things nice and legal." Lampkin looked up at Bideau's son, who seemed to fill the door.

Whipple signed the documents as the representative of C. Lampkin Corporation, in a tight, barely legible script. Lucas Bideau signed as the witness. Rufus Bideau smiled his warm-cold smile and handed Whipple the flask. Whipple sipped the substance and passed it back to Rufus who took a final drink before handing it to Lampkin. "Take a swig. In fact, keep the flask as a memento."

Caleb Lampkin sipped the bourbon very slowly, savoring its quality. The spider reappeared before him, its web bigger, much bigger.

19
The First Pitch

THURSDAY CAME. True to his word, Brady had martinis at the ready along with assorted cheeses and crackers. Rose quickly drank one of the silvery delights and nodded his approval. Smyth asked for black coffee—he was there for business alone. The rest divided—some opted for martinis, others coffee. Grieger became the unofficial note taker, scribbling first about the ambiance of the host's surroundings.

Brody Brady's condominium reflected its owner—some of the furniture was old, but all of it was well cared for. "These pieces come down from my great grandparents on my mother's side," he explained to Grieger. Brady pointed to a large wooden desk with a pull-down cover and then a rocker. "My great grandma Essie sat on that rocker and watched the Pennsylvania militia march off to war against the South." Brady beamed with pride throughout the tour.

"Interesting," said Ginsberg, who had tagged along. "But I most love those pictures of you with all those Republican Presidents—you and Nixon, you and Ford, you and Reagan and even you with the first Bush."

"I did work for all of them," Brady responded.

"Wasn't there ever a Democrat?" asked the rabbi.

"Never!" Brady exclaimed with righteous indignation. "I would never work for those who would lead us down the path to socialism. Never, never, never! Only once did I even vote for a Democrat. He was running for county council, and I voted for him as a favor to a friend. Turned out he was a crook. Went to jail shortly after he took office. They're all either crooks or socialists in bed with the labor unions."

"Are you saying FDR was a socialist?" Grieger asked, as if interviewing some great statesman.

"Stop," intoned Smyth. "Where's this representative we're here to see?"

"Any moment," Brady responded.

The doorbell rang. Brady opened the door and in stepped Chris Bideau. He smiled his bright, handsome smile, apologized for being late, and presented Brady with a bottle of Chianti reserve. "A present from my daddy."

Bideau quickly moved to the center of the living room standing just in front of the granite fireplace. His six-foot-four-inch frame seemed to fill a third of the room's space. His shoulders stretched his plaid jacket to the point that Grieger wrote, "It seemed to groan like a canvas sail in a storm." The young Bideau was imposing, yet not threatening. Even Smyth seemed relaxed.

The Martini Clubbers formed a semi-circle around Chris Bideau, their eyes glued on him with a mix of fascination and suspicion. The young Bideau tugged at his striped tie, which constrained his thick, muscular neck. He declined a drink, but grinned, "After, we can talk football, if you want."

"That's where I know you from," said Grieger, who had covered sports before going over to city-side reporting. "You were that great defensive back for Goodness of God College. Why didn't you go pro?"

"Couldn't pass the physical. Got a bum right knee."

"You're also the Parrot's Caw property manager who precipitated a riot," Grieger added with a journalistic frown.

"That crazy pimp started it," Chris Bideau snapped. Then, regaining his composure, he continued. "And, yes, I am proud to say I am the property manager at Parrot's Caw. I try to give superb service. If you have any complaints, please don't hesitate to talk to me after this meeting."

"No complaints, but I do have questions," Grieger continued. "Why in the world is the Parrot's Caw property manager talking to us about a million-dollar switchgrass deal?"

"Mr. Brady didn't tell you?"

"He doesn't tell us anything until it is too late," Grieger replied. "So why don't you clear this up for us?"

"RB&S, the development company that built Parrot's Caw, is owned lock, stock and barrel by my daddy, Rufus Bideau. He is also an investor in numerous commercial projects. The "S" stands for sons. That's my brother Lucas and me. While I continue to manage Parrot's Caw, I also work on my daddy's other projects, including the switchgrass deal, as you call it."

Chris had been briefed by Rufus on what to expect during the meeting. The senior Bideau had explained that several of the members would have done their research not only about switchgrass and Verde Bioenergy, but about Rufus Bideau and sons as well. They would have discovered that everything he told Brody Brady was true. They would have found that Rufus Bideau was a successful entrepreneur who lived in a historic mansion in Stuarton. What they would not find, of course, was any reference to a recently sold five-hundred-acre farm near the city. That was Rufus Bideau's secret, the enticement that would make these men invest. Rufus had tried to do some research on The Martini Club, but there was nothing about the group on the Internet. It was not incorporated nor sanctioned by any other organization. There were no Facebook posts or even a tweet. Of course, old men don't chat on social media. Bideau, however, had found considerable material about Brody Brady.

After a brief stint as a United States Army draftee in the post-Korean War period, Brady had embarked on a career as a Washington-based television journalist. Brady switched to press spokesperson for Richard Nixon during Nixon's bid for the presidency in 1960. Some of Brady's comments amused Bideau. One report quoted Brady as saying, "When I was a reporter, I Interviewed Jack Kennedy a couple of times. He isn't smart. Dick Nixon is another matter. He is very smart. I admire him." Bideau laughed. He considered Brady too dumb to distinguish between who was smart and who was not.

When Nixon lost his presidential bid to John F. Kennedy, Brady was out of a job. Since his name appeared on the Kennedy brothers' informal blacklist, it was difficult at first to find work with private clients. Undeterred, Brady opened an advertising and public relations firm in Washington. The firm prospered by focusing on the needs of congressional Republicans. He did well enough over the next twenty years to marry and buy a gentleman's farm in the countryside of Virginia. He lost both in a contentious divorce.

Though he rose to the position of president of Businesses Organized Against Regulation, an association of lobbyists, he never regained the brief aura of importance he held during his time with Nixon. Ironically, he was not asked to join the administration when Nixon finally became president in 1969. Brady eventually sold his firm and relocated to Parrot's Caw. Now, instead of political rallies, he regularly attended meetings of The Stuarton Business Club. It offered tasty, cheap lunches and gave him the opportunity to rub elbows with "the people who mattered" in town. He told a local newspaper reporter that he chose Stuarton because the city's rapid growth offered numerous business opportunities, and he "had no intention of ever retiring."

Perfect, thought Rufus Bideau.

Though he lacked the names of the other Martini Club members, he was confident his son Chris would acquire them in short order. Once he possessed that information, the senior Bideau could understand his quarry and their motivations better. He sensed that they were bored old men who had nothing better to do than tend their wives' flowerbeds and get drunk once a month. Whatever wit and wisdom they once possessed had been drained by time. What remained were empty, useless vessels desperate to relive their glory days. *Perfect lambs,* he thought. *Yes, their clothes are cleaner and more expensive, and they certainly smell a lot better, but in reality they are not much different from Farmer Lampkin.*

20
Closing the Deal

"I AM HERE to expand on what Mr. Brady told you," Chris Bideau began. "I'm not going to tell you much more about how switchgrass will be the biodegradable fuel of the future. My mission today is to explain how we will all get rich while raising the one million dollars needed to purchase the farm that will grow enough of this plant to multiply our investment untold times." He paused, then added dramatically, "But we insiders won't have to wait 'til then. We will be able to get returns on our personal investments almost immediately."

The younger Bideau went on to explain that his father did not expect each of the club's ten members to put up one hundred thousand dollars. "Mr. Brady made it clear to my daddy that while you all are all well off, you might not have the resources to risk that kind of money—even if the project is sure fire."

Grieger half expected the pom-pom girl to burst out of Brady's bedroom and lead them all in some kind of Calypso cheer.

MAR-TEEN-NI, MAR-TEEN-NI,
MAR-TEE-NI, MAR-TEE-NI
WE-ALL-GONNA-MAKE-SO-MUCH-MONEY.

The girl did not appear, however. Oddly, this disappointed Grieger.

Chris Bideau had the group's full attention. "We are going to form an investment club. You will each be asked to pay ten thousand dollars—a sum Mr. Brady advises you all can afford. As the initial investors, you will have the sole voting rights on use of the money. Once that money is raised, the investment club will offer associate memberships to friends and relatives, so that they too can be enriched. They, however, will not have voting rights."

Bideau paused again, to let this joyous information sink in. "Each associate membership will sell for one thousand dollars. For every share sold, the seller will receive one hundred dollars. This means each of you will begin receiving an immediate return on your investment. In addition, all financial returns will be based on the size of the member's investment. We'll do this informally, among the insiders."

"Is there anything illegal about this?" asked Corrigan.

"No. As I said, this is an investment club. We won't be publicly trading shares on the stock market, and we won't run afoul of the Securities and Exchange Commission. We are selling memberships. My daddy's already checked all the rules and regulations. As an additional protection for the investors, two signatures will be required to withdraw any money from the bank account established for the investment club. Daddy recommends himself and Brody Brady as the signatories."

Displaying a heretofore hidden ability with numbers, Smyth said, "That means we have to get more than one thousand people to buy one share before we get to the one million dollars needed to close the deal on the farm."

"Nothing stops you from selling an investor two associate memberships or more," Chris responded professionally.

Still sensing hesitancy, Chris Bideau continued as his father had coached him to do. "There will be others offering these memberships, too. My daddy is prepared to reach out to his own network of associates, who will eagerly snap them up. After all, a single associate membership, purchased at this insider price, could be likened to buying a complete retirement package. Investing in a switchgrass farm is like investing in an oil well in Texas."

Brady drew the big picture for the group. "Millions of years ago, all kinds of vegetation grew up, died, got buried and ultimately changed into oil, gas and coal. They are called fossil fuels—switchgrass is a modern ancestor. The big difference is that we now know how to extract fuel from switchgrass, so we don't have to wait millions of years to use it, and the fuel is clean."

"What do we call the investment club?" asked Rose, clearly sold on the idea.

"An interesting question. My daddy suggests, 'The Burning Bush Investment Club' because we will be turning switchgrass into fuel."

"Kind of biblical," Rabbi Ginsberg noted. "Is your father a religious man?"

"He likes to think so," Chris replied.

Twenty minutes later, all ten Martini Club members had signed a paper authorizing Rufus Bideau and Brody Brady to open a bank account in the name of The Burning Bush Investment Club.

21
The Banker Intervenes

Once each of The Martini Club members bought their Burning Bush memberships at ten thousand dollars apiece, the sale of the remaining shares went surprisingly well. Nine hundred thousand was raised in just one week. They had gone straight to relatives and close friends and urged them in turn to reach out to their friends and families. Rufus Bideau even got Wilfred Longcastle, president of Stuarton's All Peoples Heritage Bank, to purchase six associate memberships in return for placing The Burning Bush Investment Club's funds at his institution. The investment, Bideau had told Longcastle, would bring a ten-fold return. Bideau hadn't expected the banker to part with a dime. He was surprised when Longcastle did.

Longcastle had never trusted Bideau, whom he considered a rogue, and had not been taken in by Bideau's sales pitch. However, the banker needed more information about the deal, and the best way to get that information was through an investment. Besides, he could well afford the six-thousand dollars, and it had already yielded a new one-million-dollar bank account as well as valuable intelligence.

Until Rufus Bideau approached him, Longcastle had been unaware that Verde Bioenergy was making inquiries about opening up a plant in the vicinity of Stuarton. Nor had he known that there was a farm with a vast amount of switchgrass to supply the plant. Longcastle wondered why such a farm would cost one million dollars. No farm in the area had sold for more than five hundred thousand dollars in the last ten years. Despite his questions, Longcastle understood well the opportunities that might emerge from a relationship with Verde and ultimately selling switchgrass in Stuarton...that is, of course, if anything Rufus Bideau had told him was true.

While Longcastle was no saint, and clearly understood the harsh realities that governed banking and investing, he believed himself to be a moral individual. Bideau, on the other hand...well, there was something dark and sinister about that man.

Longcastle also had been curious about a check the bank had recently received from the C. Lampkin Corporation paying off a destitute local farmer's mortgage plus all interest and penalties that had accrued. He thought it odd that someone like Lampkin, who he knew to be a drunk, would be conducting business as a corporation. Now he sensed a connection between Rufus Bideau's mystery farm and Lampkin's sudden ability to pay off not only the bank, but also the utilities that had been shut off due to lack of payment. The banker decided to pay Farmer Lampkin a visit.

~

Though it was still morning, Lampkin was well into a bottle of rotgut whiskey when Longcastle arrived. The farmer was seated in his porch rocker swatting at the spider that seemed to continually weave its web in endless circles around him. He was nowhere near as drunk as he had been before all his bills were paid off. He had once again become accustomed to running water, lights and other electric powered conveniences.

He expected no good from the banker's unexpected appearance. "Off my property, banker!" Lampkin reached for his rusty shotgun and leveled it at Longcastle's chest.

Always a cautious man, Longcastle tarried behind the substantial open door of his limousine. He did not think Lampkin would actually shoot him. For that matter, he questioned whether the rusty shotgun the farmer was holding could actually fire. "I just want to have a word with you, Mr. Lampkin. Your place is now mortgage free. No fear that the bank wants to take it away from you. We are happy with your money, though I do have some information that might make you a very rich man."

"You can give me that information from right where you are, and then skedaddle out of here." Lampkin did not lower his shotgun.

"I may have a buyer for your property," Longcastle said from behind the car door. "He might be willing to pay you twenty-five dollars an acre, plus an extra twenty thousand for your house."

"Too late," Lampkin answered. "Already sold it for two dollars an acre. Got all my bills paid and the right to stay in this house for the rest of my life."

Longcastle quickly calculated that the farmer's mortgage and bills came to no more than one hundred thousand. A lifelong home to live in—even a ramshackle one like this—might be worth ten thousand at most. If Verde Bioenergy is coming in, Longcastle thought, it's a steal. "And who was the generous buyer?" he asked.

"None of your damn business," the farmer snapped.

"Now, don't get mad. The change of deed has not yet been filed with the county. I just might be able to get you a better deal, but I have to know who bought you out."

Lampkin needed time to think. That damn spider seemed to be weaving its web right around his brain. It was making it hard for him to concentrate. All he really wanted was to sit in his rocking chair with a bottle and drink away the pain. He didn't like the idea of being taken for a fool, though. Maybe he had been taken. He swatted away the spider. "Rufus Bideau bought the place. Had me sign the papers right inside my living room. Can you make him give me more money?"

"I certainly will try to get someone to give you more money. Thank you for your cooperation. I will be back with a better deal for your land soon, a better deal indeed." Longcastle slipped cautiously back into his limousine and ordered his driver to take him back to his office. The banker smiled and considered whether there might be a business opportunity here.

22
A Bottle of Whiskey

RUFUS BIDEAU WAS annoyed. He had just gotten a call from Caleb Lampkin demanding that he cancel the sale of his farm.

"You cheated me!" Lampkin shouted into the phone.

Lampkin was supposed to sit on his rocker and drink himself to death, Bideau thought, not call and try to cancel the deal. "A deal is a deal," he replied coldly.

"Not if it hasn't been filed with the county clerk," Caleb shot back.

"Who told you that?" Bideau asked, annoyance turning to surprise and anger.

"None of your damn business," Lampkin snapped back.

Bideau had withheld filing the deed to reduce the possibility of anyone finding the transfer, but someone had found out. He changed his tone. "Now let's not get all riled up. Tell you what I'm going to do," he continued in a voice soft as silk. "I'm going to drive out to your place with the papers and go over them with you again, and maybe just sweeten things up a bit. Okay? No reason for things to get nasty."

Lampkin thought about it for a moment as he took a sip of rotgut whiskey. "Sure, why not. I'm a man open to negotiation."

Bideau hung up the phone and pondered the conversation for several moments. *That drunk never would have thought of going to the county clerk's office to look up a deed. There is no way he could have learned the value of his farm unless someone told him, and Brady's group has no idea who owned the farm or where to look.* Then it clicked. "The banker," Rufus exclaimed out loud. *Paying off Lampkin's mortgage was the tipoff. Damn him. Longcastle is trying to take the deal away.* "Well, he'll find it not so easy," he whispered to an empty room. "Not so easy at all." He stood up and ordered Lucas to get the car.

Maybe it was his daddy's especially nasty mood, but it seemed to Lucas Bideau that the drive to Caleb Lampkin's farm was taking much longer than it had the last time. Granted, his dad was nasty most of the time, but today he was more than nasty. Not only had he torn up Lucas's sex magazines, he'd also stomped his computer tablet to pieces. When Lucas had gotten up the courage to ask what was wrong, his daddy pulled out his pistol and placed it against his son's skull.

"Sometimes you're too much like your brother," the elder Bideau growled. "You ask too many questions. Shut up and do as you're told."

Nudging his son with the barrel of his weapon, he ordered him to stop at The Skull & Bones, a biker bar just off the Post Road where it crosses Pasture Lane.

"You want me to mess up somebody in there?" Lucas asked.

"I want you to go in there and buy two bottles of Jay McLeish's. Don't make trouble. Just buy the whiskey and leave."

"But Pa, bars don't sell bottles of whiskey. They sell shots."

"Don't you think I know that boy? I don't want you to go to a package store. It's too obvious. Here, this should help the bartender make an exception to the law." He handed his son two crisp hundred dollar bills.

Lucas knew not to ask questions. He walked up to the bar. A small group of leather-jacketed men sat at a table eating burgers and drinking beer. They looked up when he entered and immediately decided he was too big and mean looking to fool with. Lucas approached the bartender, a tall, slender man with a two-day growth of beard.

As Lucas expected, the man refused to sell him two unopened bottles of whiskey. Following his father's directions to the letter, Lucas then offered the bartender a hundred dollars for each bottle. "And if that isn't enough, I'll come over this bar and break your neck." He grabbed the bartender's arm and pulled him close against the mahogany bar top. The bikers looked up, but decided it was none of their business.

The bartender hesitated. He was used to tough bikers, who brawled and occasionally took swings at him. That was why he kept a .38 caliber revolver in an easy-to-reach shelf below the bar. But this huge muscular man in front of him didn't look like someone to be intimidated by a gun. His face carried the ugly meanness of a man who would kill without a moment's thought. Besides, he was offering two hundred dollars for two bottles of Jay McLeish's that had cost him only fifty apiece. It was a win-win. Profit and no trouble. He left the .38 on its shelf.

Lucas exited the bar quickly and headed for the car. He personally didn't care much for bourbon style whiskey. A good beer suited him better. There was nothing like downing a dozen brews at some out-of-town joint, and then announcing, "I'm gonna beat up every man in this place." He especially liked taking on the bouncers because they required more bashing. He once threw a bouncer through a plate glass window and watched him stagger away, bleeding from the head and neck. At another bar, the owner let loose a Doberman Pincher, which bit him. He snapped the dog's neck and choked the bar owner unconscious, racing off before the police arrived. No one could identify Lucas, except to describe him as a big man with a nasty temper. His father warned him never to pull such a stunt in Stuarton, where Lucas could be recognized. Unnecessary violence was bad for business.

They drove the final stretch to Lampkin's farmhouse without talking. As Rufus Bideau stepped out of the car, he motioned Lucas to join him and bring the bottles of whiskey. They were up the creaking front porch steps before Caleb Lampkin could get out of his rocking chair. The senior Bideau grasped the farmer's arm and moved him through the front door. He sat Lampkin in a chair and stood directly in front of him. He motioned Lucas to get behind the chair. Rufus looked around quickly, and noticed that the place smelled a bit better than before. *Solvency has its virtues*, he thought.

"I haven't got much time to fool with you, Lampkin," Rufus Bideau hissed.

"I thought you came here to renegotiate our contract," the farmer answered.

Bideau smiled his cold smile. "Before we get to that, let's have a nice, friendly drink together." He motioned Lucas to open one of the bottles and pulled a couple of shot glasses from his coat. He thrust one into Lampkin's hand and generously filled it with the golden brown liquid. "Let's toast to a different approach to our deal. Drink up."

Both men tossed down their drinks in a single motion. The good whiskey lingered on Lampkin's pallet, conjuring up memories of better days. He'd almost forgotten the taste of good liquor. "That was mighty obliging of you, Mr. Bideau. Now let's talk business."

"Yes, let's talk business. You made a deal with me. You signed a contract. Now you want to change the deal—who put this silly idea in your head? I negotiated with you in good faith. I paid your bills and made sure that you would have a roof over your head for the remainder of your days. And what do you do? You betray me."

Caleb Lampkin had finished only a quarter bottle of rotgut whisky thus far into the day, but tasting the good liquor made him thirsty again. Ordinarily, he'd have put away nearly a full bottle of his homemade brew by this time in the afternoon, but he'd been feeling happier since paying off his debts. Still, he loved his Panther Piss. Some West Virginia boys he'd met in the Army had showed him how to produce the drink, which averaged far better than one hundred proof after the appropriate distilling. In a few weeks' time, he'd refined the recipe. When some Navy submariners challenged him to match his Panther Piss against the Torpedo Juice they'd manufactured under the sea, he obliged and won hands down. According to the neutral GI judges, Lampkin's Panther Piss tasted better, went down more smoothly—not as much fire in the throat—and did not make you blind at the end of the day. Now, here he was sippin' on some fancy Jay McLeish's. Life certainly was looking up. But that didn't mean he was going to let this Bideau character take advantage of him.

"You tried to steal my farm from me," Lampkin snapped, noticing the black spider spinning its web just in front of him.

"Who told you your farm was worth a dime more than I offered?" Bideau demanded.

"None of your business. But our contract ain't worth a darn unless it's filed with the county clerk. So I want to renegotiate, and I know where to get help, if you don't."

"I had hoped that we could resolve this man to man. That I would drive away from here satisfied that we had dealt with each other amicably. But now I see there is no talking to you. Despite my generosity, you have turned into a whining, greedy drunk. You leave me no choice, Lampkin. Lucas, hand me the open bottle of Jay McLeish's and open the second one."

"Bideau, I'm not in the mood to sit here drinking with a man who tried to cheat me out of my farm," Lampkin said as he rose unsteadily to his feet.

"Hold him down," Rufus Bideau instructed his son.

Lucas seized Lampkin's skinny arms in a powerful grip and slammed him down in the chair. Rufus Bideau then grabbed the farmer's straw-colored hair and yanked his head backward. "Open wide." He began pouring the golden liquid down Lampkin's throat.

Lampkin struggled wildly, trying to close his mouth, but Rufus Bideau held the farmer's nose, forcing his mouth to stay open or suffocate. "Drink, drink, drink," he urged, in a warm, soothing tone. Lampkin gagged and coughed and managed to draw blood when he clawed Rufus Bideau's hand, but he was too weak. After a while, the farmer stopped resisting.

He was slowly drifting through a golden haze toward the giant web. The spider was there at the center waiting for him, preparing its poison. Somehow he always knew it would end like this. Maybe Martha would come to him now.

23
Rose Shows His Stuff

THE MARTINI CLUB's next meeting was at Mike Rose's place for the first time. It was a palatial establishment in the most affluent section of Parrot's Caw. Rose's home featured high ceilings and wide corridors that opened into a large dining room and even larger living room. He called it his great room—with vast windows that offered wide-angle views of the home's spacious garden. The walls were graced with large paintings, mostly of seductively posed women in minimal attire. As The Martini Club members entered, they were escorted past portraits of Bugsy Siegel, Meyer Lansky, Lucky Luciano and other notorious gangsters whose visions of Las Vegas turned it into the gambling capital of the United States, and Nevada into its sex capital. "Those men were heroes in their own unique way," Rose told his friends.

"Sure, if killing makes you a visionary," grunted Grieger.

"Would you today condemn the Robber Barons, who pushed the railroads across this country and helped make America the most powerful nation in the world? Plenty of Chinese workers died building those railroads. Nobody cared then. Nobody cares now," Rose answered. "Or would you condemn men who made their fortunes through slavery, like Washington and Jefferson?"

"Shit," snorted Smyth. "Where are the Picassos and the Dalis?"

"Sold them along with the rest of Moon House," Rose answered.

"Moon House? What is Moon House?" Smyth asked.

"It is the kind of place where lust and licentiousness gain free expression. A place where the needs of the flesh meet the gratification of the soul. It is a brothel. Moon House was my business and my temple, bought and paid for with loans from my parents, my wife Sophie's parents and others I would rather not mention. I sold it at a sufficient profit to allow me to live in comfort in this wonderful community."

Rose pointed toward an enormously large photograph of a three-story mansion that overlooked a sweeping circular driveway where a limousine was discharging a man in a top hat and tails. "That, my friends, is Moon House," he said in a voice filled with reverence. "You should visit it and get rid of some of your frustrations."

"I have never paid to get laid, and never will," Smyth bragged. "Nor do I harbor frustrations. Now pour the martinis, you monkey-sized Jew whore master."

Rose tensed and reflexively felt for his weapon. *No,* he thought. He stole a last glance at his beloved Moon House, turned silently and proceeded to fill each member's glass with the silvery liquid. He came to Smyth last, looked up at his hard face, smiled and proceeded to pour the martini directly on to Smyth's polished loafers. Everyone was silent, expecting Smyth to hurl the diminutive Rose across the room. Instead, Smyth just stood there looking down expressionless at his expensive, wet shoes.

"Who you calling a monkey-sized Jew, you WASP son-of-a-bitch?" Rose snarled at Smyth. "Sophie and I grew up in a shanty town in Brooklyn. We came from nothing. I drove a laundry truck. She waited tables. Then, one day, this guy Shelly who I ran some numbers for asked if I was willing to take a shot and move to Nevada. Said his friends would set me up and he'd vouch for me. We moved. We took our shot. And those mob guys were as good as my friend Shelly's word. They set me up in the whore business, as you call it. Sophie wasn't crazy about it at first. But it was legal. We told our folks we ran a motel. Eventually, I got my own place. Made a lot of money. Paid off my creditors. Even got some education…some polish. I'm living the American dream, Smyth. I'm not some cold blooded hit man, like you."

The retired CIA man broke into a wide grin. "Rose you've got more piss and vinegar than a one-eyed Somali pirate. I love you, you pint-sized bastard. But when will you people get over your hangups? I was making a damn joke. I worked with guys in the Mossad…"

Rabbi Ginsberg broke in. "Rose didn't like being called monkey-sized. It's not the Jew thing. We Jews are used to being called Jews. We just don't understand why Christians feel a need to use the term when it is irrelevant." Ginsberg got up from his chair and put his arm around Rose's shoulders. "I didn't know you were a Brooklyn boy. Me too. In that borough, we ate anti-Semites for breakfast."

Brody Brady had had enough. It was time for a change of tone. Raising his glass high, he said, "I propose a toast to the success of The Burning Bush Investment Club. It has now sold thirty thousand dollars' worth of club associate memberships and the buyers are spreading the word. I've received calls from people who are friends of relatives, people I don't even know—all want to buy in. So gentlemen, here's to The Burning Bush Investment Club. We've already collected three thousand dollars in commissions. Not bad!" Glasses were raised. "We're back in the action, back in the game."

"To The Burning Bush Investment Club," they shouted in unity and sipped their drinks.

"This just better work or I'm going to have some really pissed off family and friends," Grieger cautioned.

"It will work. No question," replied Brady, ever the optimist. "I heard through the grapevine that Wilfred Longcastle, head of All Peoples Heritage Bank—Stuarton's biggest bank—personally bought six associate memberships. We will not get hurt. I guarantee it."

24
One Dead Farmer

Sheriff Elijah Pew wrinkled his nose as he sniffed the decaying body of farmer Caleb Lampkin. "Stinks as much from alcohol as it does from death," he said to Coroner Jake Bizby, who was going over the corpse looking for answers.

"Looks like he finally drank himself to death," Bizby said, acknowledging not only the smell of alcohol but the dried vomit that often accompanied alcohol poisoning. "Can't be sure until we cut him open, but see the bluish coloring of his skin? Symptomatic of poisoning. He could have strangled on his vomit or simply stopped breathing because alcohol shuts down the autonomic nervous system. Lampkin was a drunk for the past few years, but I won't really know if that's what killed him until we do the autopsy. Right now, I'd estimate he's been dead three or four days.

"Took care of his wife before she passed. In fact, the entire Lampkin family was part of my medical practice for many years, Caleb included." Bizby continued, "After Martha died, he stopped coming. I heard rumors of his drinking. Felt sorry for the man. First his farm went, then his wife."

The laconic sheriff grunted a response as he placed latex gloves on his hands before picking up the bottle of

Jay McLeish's whiskey that lay in Lampkin's right hand. "Funny, Caleb swigging his whiskey with his right hand," he said.

"Why's that?" Bizby asked.

"He probably was left handed," Pew replied. "He's wearing a watch on his right wrist."

His training at the FBI's Academy for Law Enforcement Officers had taught Pew to look for the small things that seemed out of place. These often revealed aspects of a crime not obvious in the initial investigation. This was especially true where death was involved. "Death," the trainer had told him, "tends to freeze the senses. An investigator has to overcome that kind of paralysis. For example, the bloody hammer was clearly the lethal weapon lying next to a victim whose head was bludgeoned. But the tiny fibers at the base of that hammer indicated the killer was wearing gloves. Thus the killing was likely premeditated, not a spontaneous act of passion. This changes the direction of the investigation."

"You're absolutely right," the coroner replied. "I remember when he was a patient of mine, he always complained that the buttons on his clothes were made for right-handed people."

A second empty bottle of Jay McLeish's lay a foot away—again to Lampkin's right. "Dust these two bottles for fingerprints," he ordered the deputy who was assisting Bizby. *Odd,* he thought, *two bottles of expensive whiskey at Caleb's side, yet the trash pail is filled with cheap Sneaky Pete and other rotgut whiskey.*

The deputy, a tall, skinny girl named Ida Mae Moore, was a recent graduate of the State University Forensics Program. She had worked for the sheriff's office for less than a month. She was a quick learner, eager to pick up the things they didn't teach her in school. Now she was looking at the sheriff as if he had interrupted an anatomy lesson. "I was helping Dr. Bizby," she mustered.

"You work for me," Pew shot back. "My name's at the bottom of your paycheck. When I say jump, you ask 'how high?' No lip. Got it? That's the biggest lesson you're going to learn today, if you want to keep getting those checks and a chance to watch Bizby do his job."

Bizby, who was listening with some amusement, knew the sheriff had hired the girl not only because she was dirt cheap as a new graduate, but because she seemed bright. He wouldn't fire her unless she spilled hot coffee on him or ruined a case because of carelessness. Pew did not like carelessness.

Bizby smiled at the sheriff and said, "If you're done, I'm going to have the body taken to the autopsy room for a more thorough examination. I'll send you a report, though it's pretty clear he died from alcohol poisoning." The coroner was a soft, round man with a waistline saved from humiliation by large orange suspenders, which seemed to add lift as he rose. "Oh, there is another odd thing," he said. 'Both his arms show pre-mortem bruising around the biceps—as if someone had squeezed him real hard."

"Interesting," the sheriff said. The odd things were beginning to make him rethink the idea that Caleb had simply drunk himself to death. He pulled open a desk drawer. It was empty. Its contents were neatly piled on the desk directly above the drawer. He pulled out a second drawer. It too was empty, with its contents neatly piled above it on the desk. The drawer in the dining room table also was empty. Its contents, mostly wine bottle corks, fancy napkins, old anniversary cards and a silver flask, rested on the table above. *Was somebody looking for something?* the sheriff thought to himself.

"That's strange," Pew said aloud.

"What's strange?" Bizby inquired, as much for the girl as for himself. "That the drawers are empty?"

"In part," the sheriff replied. "But look around this place. Do you see anything neat and orderly? No, nothing but the contents of these drawers. All of them are in neat, orderly piles. That's really strange. That's not been Caleb's way since his wife died."

He turned to the deputy. "Ida, dust all the drawers and door knobs for prints. On the way back to the office, I want you to stop at liquor stores and ask whether any of them had recently sold two bottles of Jay McLeish's whisky to Caleb Lampkin." She nodded obediently.

As they exited the house, Pew looked again at the unusual tire tracks he had seen when he arrived. He always took the precaution of having all law enforcement vehicles park on a road a distance away from a potential crime scene. Driveways could tell stories, especially gravel driveways, where the tiny stones formed storage basins for used tissues, cigarette butts and tire tracks. In this case, the driveway held even more potential because it had not rained for several days. Clues had not been obliterated.

Sheriff Pew quickly noted the two sets of tracks in Lampkin's driveway. One belonged to the postal truck that had stopped there to deliver a return receipt card. The driver had found Lampkin's body. He'd immediately called 911 and unthinkingly dropped the receipt on the dining room table. The lawman had spotted it and carefully placed it in a plastic bag for later review. When questioned, the postman explained that it wasn't like

Caleb Lampkin to mail letters requiring return receipts. In fact, the farmer rarely sent letters.

The other set of tracks had been made by tires that were wide, deep and of a design found on new foreign cars. He told Ida Mae to make a plaster casting of the tracks and see if she could determine the make of the car that had left them. The local FBI office could help her with that. The girl's face brightened. She had not worked with the FBI before.

25
A Disturbing Death

Brody Brady thought his latest bit of information warranted a special meeting of The Martini Club. "I know it wasn't my turn to pour, but I felt it important to share this information with you," he told the members. "I met earlier this week with Rufus Bideau, and he told me we have sold almost one million dollars worth of memberships. The people of Stuarton have gobbled them up. My fellow members, you should be proud. The Martini Club alone has sold nearly two hundred thousand dollars' worth to our friends and relatives. We will be making them all rich soon."

"What happens next?" asked David Neville, the ever-cautious lawyer. "Shouldn't Bideau be closing the deal with our mystery farmer?"

"I'm glad you asked that question," responded Chris Bideau, whose attendance Brady had requested. "Daddy is in the process of buying the farm as we speak. The one-million-dollar agreement is nearly signed, sealed and delivered. There is a slight hitch, however. Daddy has to finish up some business with the real estate lawyer. But don't worry, by Friday The Burning Bush Investment Club should be the owner of a five-hundred-acre farm that could be worth one hundred million dollars in just a few short years. That kind of money, my friends, will buy a lot of martinis."

Ginsberg expressed the group's sentiment when he said, "I'll be glad when this is wrapped up. I've sold memberships to everyone I know, from former congregants to…well…my girlfriend, or almost my girlfriend."

The girlfriend part caught Smyth's attention. "You've got a girlfriend, rabbi? Are you allowed to have a girlfriend?"

"I'm not a Catholic priest, Gerald. I can have half a dozen girlfriends, if I want."

"Is she a nice Jewish lady? Someone from your old congregation?"

"She is not from my old congregation, and she is not Jewish. And it is none of your business."

Smyth feigned shock. "Why the secrecy? Give us a name."

Ginsberg's face flushed.

"Just tell me if you can still get it up," Smyth needled.

"That's none of your damn business either," Ginsberg snapped. "My relationships are not up for discussion."

"I've been a widower for years," Smyth continued. "I'm willing to talk about it. After all, we are true blue friends, boon buddies, whatever you want to call us."

"I call you a scumbag," Rose broke in, opening his jacket and flashing his holstered pistol as was his habit.

Sam Grieger intervened. "I noticed an interesting story in today's paper. Perhaps Chris can enlighten us."

"Certainly. If I can, Mr. Grieger," Chris responded.

Grieger paused to make sure everyone was listening before continuing. "Today's front page said a local farmer recently died of apparent alcohol poisoning. However, the article noted that the coroner was keeping the investigation open due to some unusual circumstances surrounding the farmer's death. The news report gave no details. Interestingly, this farmer owned a five-hundred-acre farm that had gone fallow. Seems the guy had all kinds of things go wrong—wife died, fields were infested, bank was close to foreclosing on his land. Could that be our farm, Chris?"

"Daddy has not told me which farmer he has been dealing with," Chris responded, honesty aglow in his face.

"Well, if it is the same farm, I have three problems," Grieger responded. "First, how do you negotiate with a dead man? Second, the land is described as filled with dry scrub and sagebrush, not switchgrass. Third, this farm doesn't sound like it is worth a million dollars."

Chris wrinkled his brow. "I can't answer all your questions right now. Daddy was dealing with a real estate lawyer. I will speak to my daddy and get back to you." He started toward the door, but Smyth blocked his way. "There is a telephone in the adjoining room. I strongly suggest you call your 'daddy,' and get some quick answers."

Chris weighed the option of tossing Smyth into the adjoining room and walking out the door. While Smyth was old, there was something still formidable about him—a darkness in his eyes. It was the same darkness Chris saw in his father's eyes. Besides, busting up Smyth might ruin the business deal. His dad would not like that. Chris decided that daddy was more dangerous than Smyth.

"I'll make the call." Chris dialed the phone.

"What?" snapped Rufus Bideau in his harsh voice.

"Trouble," Chris half whispered. "One of The Martini Club members read a story in today's paper about a farmer with five hundred acres of land dying from too much booze. Now they want to know if that's the farmer we're supposed to be dealing with. I told them I don't know. I said you are dealing with a real estate lawyer."

"Excellent work," Rufus Bideau replied, paying his son a rare compliment. "You are a smart boy. Tell our investors I will meet with them soon and will have some very good news to share."

Chris relayed the message to Smyth, who nodded his head and led the young man to the door. The Martini Club would wait for the good news.

26
A Revealing Letter

Sheriff Pew carefully withdrew from the evidence bag the mail receipt he had found at Caleb Lampkin's home. He stared at the farmer's signature and the name of the person to whom the letter was sent. The wobbly script was undoubtedly genuine, the product of a liquored hand.

He also recognized the name of the addressee, Rachel Barlow. He had first known her as Rachel Lampkin, Caleb's kid sister. He had grown up with her in Stuarton. They had gone to the same high school and knew each other casually—well enough to say hello when they passed in the hallway. He remembered her as attractive with a small waist blending into rounded hips, provocative but not overly large breasts, full lips and deep brown eyes. She was one of the smart ones who felt more comfortable with the nerds than the jocks. He was one of the jocks, happy to keep his grades just high enough to let him play varsity baseball.

That was fifteen years ago. Rachel had moved to Boston for college, and rarely returned to Stuarton. The last time she came home, she brought a husband, a child and a PhD. He, on the other hand, had gone to the city's community college and earned a two-year degree in criminal justice. He took a job with the Sheriff's Department and rose to chief deputy. When Sheriff Corey Solomon retired after twenty years, a citizens coalition asked Pew to run for the office. "We need a non-partisan sheriff's department," the leader of the coalition had told him. "And you have played it down the middle as long as we've known you." Pew ran and won easily.

It unsettled Pew to think that today he was looking up Rachel's phone number to tell her that her brother was dead and that he needed to take a look at whatever Caleb had sent her.

He dialed her number slowly. The voice on the other end was melodious. "Rachel speaking."

"Hello. This is Elijah Pew, Rachel. Maybe you remember me."

"Best pitcher and second baseman Stuarton High ever had," she replied and laughed.

"Didn't think you'd noticed," he answered with a weak smile.

"Didn't think you cared."

They chatted about their lives since high school for a couple of moments. Then the sheriff interjected, "I have some difficult news." He told her that her brother had died, apparently from alcohol poisoning, but there were some peculiar circumstances he wanted to discuss with her.

"Good God! What happened, Elijah?"

The sheriff explained much of what she already knew: her brother had fallen on hard times, his wife had died, the farm's crops had failed, the kids had gone to live with Caleb's other sister, and Caleb had taken to drink. "Two days ago, your brother drank two bottles of Jay McLeish's whiskey in quick succession. He went into cardiac arrest and died."

"His wife Martha was so young, so full of life, and then she was gone." Rachel knew her brother had been depressed ever since her death. "He could have dealt with the loss of the farm. He couldn't deal with what happened to his wife."

Pew was sympathetic, but kept the conversation focused on gathering information for his investigation. "What was in the letter he sent you? What was so important that he wanted you to sign for it?"

"It was a copy of an agreement he had signed saying he had sold the farm for two dollars an acre. It also mentioned the repayment of all his debts, including the mortgage, and his right to live in his house for the rest of his life. There was a note attached telling me to put this document in a safe place."

"Did he say who was the buyer?" Pew asked.

"Yes, it was the C. Lampkin Corporation. I thought it was odd that the company was named after my brother, but Caleb said in the note that it was all legitimate. He said this way the farm kept his name even if he didn't keep the farm. It had been in our family for more than three generations."

"Who signed for the corporation?" Pew pressed.

"A man named Gideon Whipple."

"Was the document witnessed?"

"Yes. The witness was someone named Lucas Bideau."

27
An Exchange of Gifts

Deputy Ida Mae Moore found three places that sold liquor on the roads that linked Stuarton to Caleb Lampkin's farm. The first was Bob's Liquor, a store in a strip mall just outside the city limits. The second was Wally's Superstore, the anchor in a shopping mall that contained everything from a pet care store to a beauty salon. The last was The Skull & Bones, a biker bar that advertised, "Half-Price Cold Beer and Full-Bodied Hot Women."

At Bob's Liquor, Ida Mae saw a skinny little man sitting behind a counter reading a horse racing scratch sheet. He barely looked up when she entered.

"You Bob?" she asked.

"Yep, deputy," he said. "Which is it this time—Widows and Orphans Fund or Injured Troopers Endowment?"

"Neither, I want to know if you sold two large bottles of Jay McLeish's whiskey to someone recently."

"That's easy. No. Ran out of McLeish's two weeks ago and haven't been able to get a delivery."

She pulled out a picture of Caleb Lampkin. "Ever seen this man?"

"Sure," Bob answered, "but he buys rotgut. Never seen him buy a bottle of Jay McLeish's."

"Thanks," Ida Mae said, pocketing the picture. She turned and left. Bob went back to his scratch sheet. She wondered where the horses were running since there wasn't a track within a hundred miles.

Her next stop was Wally's. A bargain shopper's paradise, it overflowed with middle-class necessities, tastes and desires. Rows of smart phones beckoned to those in need of constant communication. Plastic-wrapped steaks, chops and other meat-eater delights vied for consumer attention along a butchers' wall. Ida Mae, though, was focused on only one thing—finding Wally's liquor section. She found it in a far corner, beyond the prescription drugs and housewares. It had a modest display of options compared to the number of enticements offered elsewhere in the store.

Finding no one to assist her in the liquor section, she slowly worked her way toward the electronics department. There she found a Wally's "associate," as they were called, who directed her to the gun counter. "They also handle liquor," the girl said.

A young man with a military haircut greeted her at the gun counter. "Hi deputy, can I help you? We have some fine official firearms."

"I'm interested in liquor," she replied.

The young man laughed. "A bit early for drinking, don't you think, ma'am?"

"Not funny. I need to know if you sold two of your largest bottles of Jay McLeish's to a single individual in the past two weeks. This is a police investigation."

"I can check for you." He plugged some information into a computer. After a moment, he said, "Doesn't look like it. Jay McLeish's sales have been brisk, but no two big bottles sold to one individual at one time."

Ida Mae reached inside her jacket and pulled out one of her photos of Caleb Lampkin. "Seen this guy before?"

The young man looked hard. "No, Ma'am. But if you want to give me your phone number, I'll have our people check our security tapes, and I'll call you."

Ida Mae pulled out her business card. "This has my office number. Don't bother to call, if you don't see him on your tapes." The young man looked hurt.

A short drive took the deputy to her third and final stop, The Skull & Bones. It was shortly after noon. Once inside, she found two men sitting at the end of the bar, sipping beer between bites of substantial hamburgers. Gray mixed with the black in their beards, giving the impression that their best years were probably far behind them. They stared at her quizzically, mumbled something to each other, and both smiled.

Harmless, Ida Mae thought.

She was more interested in talking to the man behind the bar. He was tall, thin and with a two days growth of beard. He turned to look at her. "Yeah?"

"I'm Deputy Sheriff Ida Mae Moore," she said, trying to sound authoritative.

The tall man looked at her for a moment. "We ain't violating no laws. My license is current, so what do you want?"

"You the owner?"

"Yeah."

"What's your name?"

"John Stokes."

"I want to know whether you sold a man two bottles of Jay McLeish's recently."

"This ain't no liquor store, lady. I sell shots, not unopened bottles. That's against the law."

"I'm not looking for license violations, but I saw a rat and some roaches as I walked in. I could call the Health Department. They could close you down. Personally, Mr. Stokes, I'm not interested in closing you down. I just need to know whether you sold two bottles of McLeish's."

The tall man looked at her hard. "Ain't no rats or roaches in here."

"That's what you say. I checked this place out with Health before coming here. You've had five violations in the past two years for lack of cleanliness. The Sheriff's office records show at least three prostitution arrests were made here. We might have to have a deputy drop by every couple of hours to check on things, if you don't cooperate."

"I don't want no trouble. You promise no trouble, I might remember something."

"Deal," Ida Mae replied. "So what might you remember?"

"About two weeks ago, a big guy comes in here—I mean a really big guy—six foot four, maybe two hundred and sixty pounds, mostly muscle. He wanted to buy two big bottles of McLeish's. I told him we don't sell liquor by the bottle. It's not legal. He said how about a two-hundred-dollar gift, and you make me a gift of two big bottles of McLeish's? That's twice what I pay for two bottles of the stuff, so I said okay. Besides, he looked like the type you don't want to cross."

Bingo, the deputy thought. Aloud, she asked, "You have any security camera footage of this guy?"

"Sorry, we erase the video once a week."

She took out one of the photos of Caleb Lampkin. "You ever see this man?"

"He looks like some guy who once tried to get my customers to buy him a drink. They kicked his ass and might have done more, if I hadn't booted him out. Any more questions? If not, I'd appreciate you leaving. Uniforms in here are not good for business."

Ida Mae obliged.

28
Whipple Has a Problem

Gideon Whipple's office was located in an old business condominium that housed two dentists, a doctor, and a practitioner of holistic medicine who sold exotic herbs, spices and liquids derived from ancient recipes. Right next to Whipple's law practice was an insurance company of dubious credibility. Its rates were low and its rate of response to claims even lower.

Insurance companies. Damn snake oil salesmen, Sheriff Pew thought as he bounded up the stairs that led to Whipple's second-floor suite. Upon entering, he immediately was hit by the overwhelming scent of cheap but provocative perfume emanating from a slight young woman who was sitting behind the reception desk. She had the beauty of youth—bright eyes and taut, fresh skin that had yet to yield to the inevitable ruts and grooves of time.

She smiled up at Pew. "May I help you?"

"Sheriff Elijah Pew. I'm here to see Gideon Whipple."

"Do you have an appointment, sheriff?"

"No, this is police business. It is urgent I talk to him."

"Unfortunately, he is in with a client right now, and can't be disturbed."

"Young lady," Pew replied, leaning toward her and placing his hands on her desk. "It wasn't a question. Buzz him now please. Tell him the sheriff must speak with him immediately, or I'll march him over to the lockup and we can talk over there."

The receptionist reddened and picked up the intercom. "I'm sorry to interrupt, Mr. Whipple, but Sheriff Elijah Pew is here and says he must see you immediately."

"Tell him I just need a minute. My client is leaving."

Pew nodded as the message was relayed.

A moment later, the door to Whipple's office opened, and a tall, dark man emerged. He stared at Pew for a long moment. Pew felt the hair on the back of his neck rise. The man nodded slightly, then moved swiftly down the flight of stairs.

"Who was that?" Pew asked the receptionist.

"That was Mr. Rufus Bideau."

Gideon Whipple appeared at the door and motioned the sheriff into his office. He was wearing a dark brown suit that hung loosely from his narrow body. His complexion had a gray pastiness to it. His shiny, bald head glowed in the light of the fluorescents overhead. "What can I do for you, sheriff? I'm a busy man but always have time to help the law."

Pew followed Whipple into his office and closed the door. Whipple slumped into a worn chair behind a desk filled with stacks of papers. An ancient picture frame hung on the wall behind him, announcing that Gideon Whipple was indeed duly accredited to practice law in the state. Whipple motioned the sheriff to a chair.

"No, thank you. I'll come right to the point, counselor. I need some answers. Who owns the C. Lampkin Corporation?"

Whipple eyed Elijah Pew and decided he did not like what he saw. Though Pew was only average height, no more than five foot ten, his solid build and hard grey eyes fit the lawyer's image of a typical lawman. Pew looked tough, maybe ruthless. The lawman's body language indicated he'd be quick to go physical. The holstered pistol at Pew's waist added to Whipple's concerns.

"I represent the corporation, but I am not authorized to reveal its principals."

Rufus Bideau had instructed Whipple to offer no information about the C. Lampkin Corporation to anyone. Since Whipple was accustomed to following Bideau's instructions to the letter, Whipple stood his ground. Bideau frightened him. There was an undertone of pent up violence about the man. Bideau's son Lucas was even more intimidating. Whipple had once seen Lucas crush a puppy to death, just for peeing on his shoe. Whipple tolerated the situation because Bideau paid well...very well. He also was concerned how Rufus would react if he told him he would no longer represent him.

"That won't do," Pew answered leaning over Whipple's desk. "I'm investigating the possible murder of Caleb Lampkin, who recently transferred complete ownership of his farm to the C. Lampkin Corporation."

Whipple squirmed in his chair. "I'm sorry, sheriff. I am not at liberty to reveal the owner of the corporation."

"Then it's just one person?"

"I can't say that either."

Sheriff Pew let a moment of silence pass, giving Whipple time to squirm. The lawyer was clearly not accustomed to dealing with law enforcement. That made sense since he was a real estate lawyer. What Pew didn't realize, was that Whipple was less concerned about the law than whether the sheriff or the Bideau family posed more of a physical threat.

"Then we have a big problem, Mr. Whipple." Pew finally said. "Your fingerprints were found in the home of the deceased. Tell me how they got there."

"I was there for the sale of the Lampkin property to the C. Lampkin Corporation."

"Did you kill Farmer Lampkin?"

Whipple's face blanched. "I didn't kill anyone. For God's sake, I've never killed anyone in my life! I wouldn't even know how to go about it."

"Then what were your fingerprints doing on the murder weapon?" the sheriff pressed, fudging the truth slightly. "Caleb Lampkin died of alcohol poisoning after having liquor forced down his throat. Your prints were on a silver flask near his body. Can you explain that?"

"I had a drink from that flask after we signed the contract, but that doesn't mean I killed him. He was alive and well when I last saw him." Whipple was now visibly sweating.

"We may have to let a jury decide that," Pew pressed on. "It doesn't have to come to that, of course, if you're willing to cooperate. Let me ask one more time. Who is the principal behind the C. Lampkin Corporation?"

The lawyer swallowed hard. "I must consult with my client." He reached for his phone.

Pew slammed his hand on top of Whipple's, preventing him from lifting the receiver. "Pick that up, and I will immediately charge you with murder, handcuff you and throw you in my lockup. And just so you know, it's currently filled with drunks, thieves and perverts. Now, who is the principal of the C. Lampkin Corporation?"

"I can't tell you. Believe me. I would if I could...but I can't." Though Whipple was genuinely frightened by the lawman, he decided the Bideaus were more terrifying than the sheriff. "Listen, I urgently need to relieve myself. The bathroom is in the reception area outside my office and the C. Lampkin Corporation file is open on my desk. I can't help what you see while I'm gone."

Whipple leaped to his feet and exited the room. The sheriff quickly went through the file. The second page identified the principal of the C. Lampkin Corporation as Rufus Bideau.

29
The Game's Afoot

Rufus Bideau leaned back in his chair and smiled. It had been a good day for The Burning Bush Investment Club. Its members had completed the sale of one million dollars' worth of memberships. Caleb Lampkin was no longer a nuisance. Everything was in place to acquire the C. Lampkin Corporation with the cash that sat in Wilfred Longcastle's bank. All it would take was his signature and Brady's to issue the check. Until now, Bideau had avoided meeting with The Martini Club. He wanted to be sure all the money was in place and that Longcastle's attempt to figure out what was happening had led him nowhere.

He reached for the phone. "Brady, it's Rufus. Sorry I wasn't able to get back to you sooner. Tying up loose ends took a bit of time. It all looks good now. We're ready for the voting members of the investment club to approve the purchase of the farm. This must be done quietly, without fanfare. No martinis. I suggest the day after tomorrow. That will give everyone time to get their calendars in order, but little time for news to leak out. The meeting shouldn't take more than an hour."

"Okay," Brady replied. "It's a bit tight, but considering what's at stake, I'm sure we can get all the boys together."

"Excellent. Let's meet at 2:00 p.m. at the Stuarton Plaza. I'll rent a small conference room."

Bideau planned to have his sons Lucas and Chris attend, in case of any trouble. Chris would try to keep the waters smooth. If that didn't work, Lucas would bust a head or two. It shouldn't come to that, Bideau thought. I've got my story in place. Yes, the crazy old farmer who drank himself to death did own the farm at one point, but it had been transferred to a corporation.

Bideau continued to review his story. As the representative of the farm's purchaser, I dealt with the real estate attorney. I have no knowledge of the beneficiaries. Of course, there was only one…me. He chuckled at the thought. He would tell The Martini Club—meeting as the decision-making members of The Burning Bush Investment Club—that his sources in the mayor's office had heard that the permitting and zoning changes necessary to start the switchgrass-to-ethanol plant were going smoothly—all top secret. The plant would be up and running inside of two years. The meeting would end, and the clueless old men would go back to their martini drinking, happy as frogs in a pond.

30
A Touch of Dante

THE MEETING WENT just as Rufus expected. First, he preached the virtues of venture capitalism. Then, for the windup, he quoted Dante's Virgil. "Fame is not for the man who lies under covers and sits on feathers; and those who use up their lives without fame leave as little trace of themselves in the world as smoke does in the air or foam in water. So, rise up and master your exhaustion with the spirit, which wins every battle... You must ascend a higher ladder still...If you understand, act to your advantage." He paused for theatrical impact, then added, "You are acting now to your advantage."

The senior members of The Burning Bush Investment Club broke into cheers and voted unanimously to pay one million dollars to purchase the five-hundred-acre farm owned by the C. Lampkin Corporation. Rufus smiled. *The fools,* he thought. It was time to mingle and chat cheerfully with those he had so easily deceived.

Their inquiries were cursory, dwelling on the technicalities of deed transfer and switchgrass planting. Neville suggested that The Burning Bush Investment Club should incorporate. Others desired to visit the farm. In due time, Bideau told them. Some had done research and were eager to apply their recently acquired knowledge of switchgrass farming.

Rufus had champagne brought in for a toast. "To the members of The Martini Club, or should I say The Burning Bush Investment Club."

Gerald Smyth broke in. "Before we drink, I once more request our noble clergyman, Rabbi Nathan Ginsberg, give the Jewish blessing over the wine."

"I would be delighted," Ginsberg responded. "I understand why a man with your history feels a need to call for as many blessings as he can. I have learned over the years that while people need to thank God, God does not need their thanks. His needs are beyond our comprehension."

"Then why pray to him?" Bideau inquired.

"Praying is not to please God. Praying is for the joy and comfort it brings you. Besides, what is lost in praying to God? If there is no caring God, it doesn't matter. If there is, maybe all those prayers will count for something. There really is nothing to lose."

Ginsberg asked everyone to rise. They prayed together. The members downed their champagne and returned to their seats. Bideau refrained from drinking until everyone was back in their chairs. Then he took small, controlled sip to appear collegial.

Bideau had never met any of the members of The Martini Club, except for Brody Brady. He had assumed they would all be like Brady—shallow, one dimensional old men who had achieved just enough money and power to give them comfortable retirements and, perhaps, a small mention in *The Washington Post* obituary page when their time came. They had tired of golf and become gullible in their boredom.

To Bideau's surprise, even Brady had turned out to be more than he had assumed. Yes, Brady had lost all the big gambles of his life. He was overmatched in marriage, and ended up divorced. He lacked the ruthlessness to be a true success in business. Even Brady's body, while large in size, betrayed him with a bad heart. *Brady should have taken his life or become a drunk like Caleb*, Bideau thought. *Instead, he chirps and dances and persuades people that all is well. He's a fool, yet not a fool.*

If Bideau had any capacity for empathy, it would be for Brody Brady...but he had none. In the end, Brady would be fleeced like all the rest. After all, the sheep were there for the wolves. It was in the nature of things.

Gerald Smyth, on the other hand, was something else. He remained a wolf. Bideau sensed a kindred blackness in him, but not so intense and dark as his. A conscience remained. Smyth had been touched by evil, but not fully embraced by it.

Then, there was the strange rabbi. He was clearly intelligent, yet there was something irritating about him.

"That quotation by Dante's Virgil was, shall I say, interesting," Ginsberg had said to him earlier in the night. "Virgil and Dante were deep in Christian Hell when the great poet made that little speech."

"I felt it appropriate," Bideau had replied weakly. *At least the rabbi got the joke.*

Ginsberg, Bideau recognized, was more than a peddler of liturgy and imagined beliefs. He talked about mankind's need to have a God that not only established ethical and moral boundaries, but also forced human beings to make choices between right and wrong. Bideau wondered if Ginsberg might be good for some future conversations.

31
The Evidence Mounts

Deputy Ida Mae Moore, Stuarton's newly hired forensic assistant, could hardly contain herself as she knocked on the door leading to Sheriff Elijah Pew's office.

"Come in."

Ida Mae opened the door with more caution than the situation required. In the last month, she had become somewhat better acquainted with the sheriff's moods. She had learned that barging into his office invariably led to a roar of "What the hell do you want? Didn't they teach you how to knock? I've got more important business on my desk than whatever it is you want to tell me." This time she knocked, and said she had something to tell him that almost certainly was more important than anything he had on his desk.

"I've got some terrific information to share, sir. Three things actually."

"All right, so tell me," Pew answered looking at her somewhat bemused. She was gangly tall with a burst of red hair. Intelligent green eyes peered out from her youthful face, but her lips were too straight and too thin to make her truly pretty. Taken all together, though, she was an attractive young woman, Pew decided.

"The FBI report came in on the tire casts. They came from a late model Mercedes sedan. There are only two of this make in Stuarton. One belongs to Mr. and Mrs. Phillip Montique, a retired couple who live in a mansion up on the hill. They both are in their eighties and have been vacationing in France for the past three months. The other belongs to Rufus Bideau, the real estate financier who lives off Fifth and Main in that three-story, antebellum house people always stare at."

"Nice work," the sheriff said. "Anything else?"

"Yes," Ida Mae replied, unable to contain a large smile. "Doctor Bizby, the coroner, pointed out to me in the autopsy that the red marks on both of Mr. Lampkin's arms, when looked at through a magnifying glass, contained palm and fingerprints. The hands that did this were so strong, they left clear images on his skin." Ida Mae was enjoying the spotlight, and paused for effect.

"So?" Pew said, impatiently urging her on with a "hurry up" hand gesture.

"So I photographed the fingerprints and asked the FBI to run comparisons. They came back to a Lucas Bideau, who was arrested two years ago on a charge of domestic violence. The charges were later dropped. His last known address is the same as that of Rufus Bideau. And that fits into the third thing. You know The Skull & Bones, that biker bar off the Post Road?"

"Yes," Pew replied more patiently than before. "I've had the pleasure of making numerous arrests there. The owner is a guy named John Stokes."

"That's the man I talked to," Ida Mae continued. "He said he gave two large bottles of Jay McLeish's to a real big, mean looking guy a couple of weeks ago. Mr. Stokes said he wanted you to understand it was a gift, not a sale–that the big guy gave him two hundred dollars as a return gift."

The sheriff laughed. "Didn't know it was gift giving time."

"Unfortunately, Mr. Stokes erased the security footage, so we don't know what the big man looks like. He did see him get into a big Mercedes, though."

"Lucas is Rufus's son." The sheriff stared at Ida Mae for a long moment, then moved swiftly around his desk and placed a large kiss on his assistant's cheek. "You may be worth every penny I pay you. Now scoot back to your desk, get a photo of Lucas Bideau. There's got to be one in the files. Show it to the bartender. Then get back here and write up everything you've told me in proper police form...and do not go beyond the facts. I don't want to catch you jumping to any conclusions. That's my job."

As instructed, Ida Mae half ran from the sheriff's office. She didn't know whether to be amazed or delighted by the kiss. She decided she was both.

32
Adding Things Up

THE SHERIFF SAT behind his oversized desk, marshaling the evidence gathered in the Caleb Lampkin case. He rocked back and forth in the big swivel chair his wife bought him when he was first elected. He pulled a fresh yellow writing pad toward him and grabbed a pencil sharpened to needle thinness. It was a leftover from his last campaign, when he gave out pencils emblazoned with DO THE WRITE THING—RE-ELECT PEW SHERIFF. Corny, but effective.

He began his list.

1. The Jay McLeish's whisky bottles lay on the wrong side of Lampkin's body.
2. Ida Mae found the fingerprints of Rufus and Lucas Bideau on the bottles.
3. The biker bartender recognized the photo of Lucas Bideau as that of the man who bought two bottles of Jay McLeish's from him.
4. Both Bideaus' fingerprints were found all over the farmer's living room. Rufus's were on the silver flask along with Whipple's. Note: the flask might have been left during an earlier visit, possibly at the signing of the sale agreement.

5. The FBI identified the driveway tracks. They belong to the same make and model Mercedes owned by Rufus Bideau.
6. The contract sent to Lampkin's sister was witnessed by Lucas Bideau.
7. The papers on Gideon Whipple's desk identified the sole owner of the C. Lampkin Corporation as Rufus Bideau.
8. Lucas Bideau's fingerprints were on Caleb Lampkin's arms. Bruising strongly suggests Lucas Bideau was holding Lampkin very tight just before he died, according to the coroner.

Eight raised a question. If Lucas was holding Lampkin, who was pouring the whiskey down the farmer's throat? It had to be Rufus, but there was no proof…or was there? *What if somebody was trying to force liquid down my throat?* Sheriff Pew thought. *What would I do? I'd close my mouth. If I closed my mouth, what would my attacker do? Hold my nose. Yes, that's exactly what he'd do to force open my mouth.*

Pew reached for the phone and called the coroner.

"What's on your mind, Elijah?" said the voice at the other end.

Caller ID, the sheriff thought. "What can you tell me about Caleb Lampkin's nose?"

"Funny you should ask," Coroner Bizby replied. "I found broken blood vessels there, not like the drinking kind. More like someone squeezed too hard. I also found something interesting under his fingernails—tiny bits of skin. Preliminary analysis shows it's not his."

"Maybe it came from the person holding Lampkin's nose," Pew suggested.

"I leave such speculations to you, sheriff. I sent everything over to Ida Mae for some research. Maybe the person's DNA will show up in one of the law enforcement databases."

"See if you can lift prints off the sides of Caleb's nose."

"Will do," the coroner responded, and hung up.

Pew called Ida Mae next. "Anything on that skin Bizby sent over?"

"The skin had traces of blood," she answered. "While there was nothing in our databases matching any of the DNA, the blood characteristics matched those found in a very old accident file for Rufus Bideau. I would feel more certain that it was Mr. Bideau's DNA, if we had something to match it against."

"Check the mouth of the silver flask we found at Lampkin's place for DNA samples. Also, Bizby is seeing if he can get any fingerprints off the sides of Lampkin's nose. If he does, he will send them to you for comparisons with any in our records." Pew slammed down the phone.

He still was puzzled. He was now sure Rufus Bideau and his son had murdered Lampkin, but what was their motive? Why would Bideau buy an old, used-up farm, even at a fair price? Nothing was adding up. There had to be something more. Why was this farm worth a murder?

33
Daddy and the Boys

THE FACT THAT his calls to Rufus Bideau had gone unanswered for several days worried Brody Brady. He had expected to hear more about the forthcoming construction of the Verde Bioenergy plan—but nothing, not even a wink or a nod.

Brady was finally able to track down Chris Bideau at the Parrot's Caw property management office. Chris greeted him with a handshake and a bear hug. "I will never forget that stripper you sent my way, Brady. At least I can laugh about it now."

"I am gratified to hear that," Brady responded. "But that's not why I am here. Have you heard anything more about the switchgrass plant?"

"Not a word," the youngest Bideau answered truthfully. "Have you talked to my daddy?"

"I have tried calling and emailing him, even stopped by his office. No luck. He seems to have vanished like a puff of smoke."

Chris began to feel uncomfortable. Whenever his daddy disappeared, someone or something usually got hurt. "Have you spoken to Lucas?"

"He was at your father's office, but all he did was grunt that he had no idea where your father was or how to get in touch with him. He practically threw me out of the place."

"Lucas can be a bit physical. Best to keep your distance," Chris advised. "I usually put this on when I meet with him..." With a hint of humor, Chris tapped his old Goodness of God football helmet, a memento he kept on his desk.

Chris recalled when he and Lucas were children. Lucas had taken a particular pleasure in pummeling him. Once, Lucas even attempted to put him in the oven. Luckily, their mother stopped him just in time. The pummeling continued until shortly after Chris reached seventeen. He had learned from his confrontation with daddy that the only way to stop abuse was to hit back. The next time Lucas punched him, Chris responded with a right to the jaw that knocked Lucas off his feet. Lucas got up and kicked Chris in the groin. Chris doubled over, and Lucas hit him on the back. Despite the pain, Chris straightened up, seized Lucas around the waist, lifted him off his feet and hurled him down a nearby flight of stairs. Lucas didn't move for several seconds. Finally, he looked up, blood dripping from his nose. "So I guess little brother's all grown up now. One day I'll bust your ass for good. Daddy told me so, and he likes me better than you."

That probably was true. Lucas looked and acted like their dad. Chris favored their mother in looks and temperament. The divorce gave his mother custody of Chris and visitation rights with Lucas, who lived with his father. Rufus Bideau tolerated Chris more than loved him, though he always had words of praise for Chris's academic achievements. "Lucas doesn't have your brains. I'll need those brains. Can't think of everything myself," he once told his son.

After Chris graduated from college, his father put him to work as the property manager for Parrot's Caw. Lucas served a different role as a kind of man Friday, bodyguard and enforcer. Lucas would visit his mother only on rare occasions. He found her too soft, too kind, too weak. Their time together was always strained. He couldn't understand why daddy kept sending her money. One day he asked.

"Good lawyer," Rufus Bideau had responded briskly.

Lucas didn't buy it, but he knew not to press the point. If the old man had any soft spot, it was for his ex-wife.

34
Some Things Become Clear

BRADY LEFT PARROT'S Caw and headed for the office of the one man he believed would have some answers, banker Wilfred Longcastle III.

The two-story rust brick building that housed All Peoples Heritage Bank was draped in a thick layer of dark green ivy. It had taken decades to grow, and bestowed upon its host an aura of stability and permanence. The residents of Stuarton could trust All Peoples Heritage Bank. It was safe. Inside, a dozen tellers worked behind a carved wooden barricade topped with bulletproof glass. Its only entrance required a special code that was revised weekly.

All Peoples was robbed only once, in the early 1930s, when Jessie and Miranda, fans of Bonnie and Clyde, entered the lobby with guns blazing. No one was seriously hurt, but the ceiling, one wall and an old plush chair still carried the scars of the holdup. To this day, the chair remains in the center of the main floor as a permanent memorial to the event—each of its bullet holes circled with indelible red marker. A small brass plaque sits on its cushion explaining the bank's brush with violence. It notes that the bandits got away with twenty-five-hundred dollars in cash, and that teller Mollie Magnus was the only person injured. She was cut by flying glass and given the rest of the week off to recover.

Wilfred Longcastle's great grandfather and namesake was said to have taken refuge beneath a large oak desk when the shooting began. Somehow he managed to call the police. He was rewarded for his bravery with a promotion that ultimately propelled him to the bank's presidency.

Longcastle's great grandson, and the bank's current president, was ensconced on the building's elegant second floor at the end of a long hallway. He sat behind a large roll top desk that his father had used during his tenure as president.

Welcoming Brady into his office, Longcastle motioned toward a formal, red silk wingback chair. It was clearly an antique, so Brady sat close to the edge, ignoring his discomfort in the pursuit of information.

"Mr. Longcastle, let me get right to the point. Like you, I am an investor in The Burning Bush Investment Club. It is no secret that our success in this venture is contingent upon the construction of a plant here in Stuarton that would convert switchgrass to ethanol. I am given to understand that negotiations are under way between the mayor and a major corporation to establish this plant. However, for the past three weeks, I've heard nothing about its progress."

"Nor have I," Longcastle responded. "What's more, I have talked to the mayor. He claims no knowledge of such a plant or negotiations to erect one." Longcastle paused to let the words sink in. "I think we have been duped, Mr. Brady."

Brady began to sweat. "That can't be," he stammered, "The Burning Bush Investment Club just bought the Caleb

Lampkin farm for one million dollars. Rufus Bideau is one of the richest men in Stuarton. He assured me these negotiations were concluding, that he had sources close to both parties telling him the deal was a certainty. Verde Bioenergy just closed a similar deal to build a plant in Victorton, Iowa.

"Yes, the Victorton deal is true," Longcastle said very calmly, having seen financial panic many times during his professional life, "but, I'm sorry to say, the story spun by Bideau about a Stuarton plant is just that—a story."

Brady, whose back had been as straight as the chair in which he was sitting, slumped. Even before he'd walked into the bank, he'd sensed that something was wrong.

"Incidentally," Longcastle continued, "I had a visit from the sheriff this morning. He wanted to know why Bideau bought Caleb Lampkin's farm. I told him I had no idea. It wasn't good for much, but Bideau seemed to have paid a fair price for it and gave farmer Lampkin the right to live there for the rest of his life, which, unfortunately, turned out to be not very long."

The banker paused for another moment to let Brady digest what he had just been told. "The sheriff also told me that the C. Lampkin Corporation, which sold you the farm, is owned lock, stock and barrel by Bideau. That farm, as you were told, was purchased to supply switchgrass to the fictional Stuarton Verde plant. I have no idea why he bought the farm under a corporate name, except maybe to cloud his interest in it."

Brady shifted uncomfortably in his uncomfortable chair. "I know why. It was all part of his scheme to swindle a lot of folks out of one million dollars. The Burning Bush Investment Club now owns a worn out farm for which it paid double or triple the fair asking price. For all I know, it's worth nothing." The realization caused Brady's weak heart to start beating rapidly. "What do I tell my friends? I talked them into this."

Longcastle shrugged. "We were all duped." The banker silently reminded himself that he'd made his investment just to keep an eye on Bideau. "At least at a thousand dollars per associate membership, the losses for each investor should be manageable even if they purchased a few memberships."

"Mr. Longcastle, perhaps you've forgotten that many of my friends live on their retirement income. We may have done well in our professional lives, but in retirement a few thousand dollars is not a sum to be dismissed."

"True. Maybe you could sue Bideau," the banker suggested halfheartedly. It wasn't that Longcastle lacked sympathy for these investors; it was just that he'd seen it all before and could never understand man's obsession with financial risk and inability to recognize when something was too good to be true. "Next time, Mr. Brady, tell them to leave their money in the bank."

Brady stood up slowly, feeling a growing tightness in his chest. He shook Longcastle's hand and left.

The banker picked up the phone. "Sheriff, I know why Rufus Bideau bought Caleb Lampkin's farm."

35
Love and Understanding

NATHAN GINSBERG FELT good. He stretched and looked across his comfortable bed at the sleeping Mary Latham. She had given him a night of sex that made him wonder whether he'd missed something during his years with Beth. No, he decided…this was just different.

Maybe women developed new sexual expertise with age. Mary had assumed various positions during that evening's intercourse, which surprised and pleased him. She had given him oral sex, and moved her tongue in amazing ways. A completely different experience, he thought. Until Mary, Nathan had known no other woman than his wife. He had been celibate since her death. Perhaps his lust had been pent up for so long that once released, it burst forth in extraordinary orgasms.

Mary opened her eyes, rolled toward him and looked up. "I always heard Jewish men were passionate," she said with a smile, resting her head on his chest. "I guess that especially applies to rabbis."

"It comes from three thousand years of practice," he responded with a grin.

Perhaps it was the Jewish guilt thing, but Ginsberg began to talk about his years with Beth, their children Joseph and Miriam, and his time preaching to a congregation that showed up mostly for the High Holy Days. "There are all kinds of Jews," he explained. "You're most likely to have seen the ultra-orthodox on TV. They are the most colorful—the men wear the black coats and hats and beards and the women dress in baggy clothes and wigs so as not to excite the men."

"After a night with you, I can see why," Mary interrupted with a laugh.

Nathan laughed, too, then brushed her flowing hair and continued. "Then there are the rest of us, the vast majority. We come in all colors, shapes, sizes and attitudes. We form what I like to think of as a Jewish civilization with the one-God belief at its core, but with great diversity on how we practice our Judaism. Some are what I call bagels and lox Jews. They define their Judaism by what they eat. They simply love the food of their ancestors—though more often than not it's actually the food of their Eastern European heritage rather than of ancient Israel. Then there are the High Holiday Jews, the ones I loved to preach to. They come a few times a year just to share the ritual and companionship of other Jews and hopefully to dwell on their rabbi's remarks. Finally, there are the secular and atheist Jews. Secular Jews don't think much about their religion. They only know they are Jews because their parents told them so. The atheists spend much of their time justifying their atheism. They just can't get away from Jewish guilt. Some even go to High Holiday services just to be with other Jews. There is one other group. They don't identify themselves as Jews at all. They even may think they're Catholics or Protestants, but others label them as Jews. The Nazis made that point most recently. I think the memory of the Holocaust unites us all."

"And which kind of Jew are you, rabbi?" Mary asked.

"I am all of the above—except for the black hats and the atheists. I believe in one God. I love the ritual. I love the food—from white fish to pita bread. I love the companionship of fellow Jews, and I love to preach. I also believe in a Jewish tradition, which suggests that as the chosen people, we have the obligation to repair the world—to make it a better place."

She kissed him lightly on the lips. There were tears in her eyes. "The man I married also was deeply involved with religion, but in a very different way."

"My parents were fallen away Catholics—agnostics, I guess, not sure that there was a God—single or in a trinity. We were what you call secular. We lived in California, mostly in the San Francisco area. It was easy to doubt in a place filled with free thinkers. I went to The University of California at San Pablo, where I majored in Art History and minored in Religion. I met a man there. He was tall, handsome, well built and smart, very smart. He was one of the youngest assistant professors at the university. He had majored in Western religions and written his PhD dissertation on the non-canonical gospels. When he lectured, he drew you in completely. It was as if he had lived through the development of these religions, and he could take you there, back in time. You could feel the gods and the demons when he talked about them. They were in a conflict that would be resolved only when good defeated evil or evil defeated good throughout the universe. We humans were some of the pawns in this struggle, arbitrarily picked to play roles determined by these cosmic forces."

"He sounds like a closet Calvinist, believing in a form of predestination," the rabbi said.

"At the time, I thought he simply wanted to make religion more exciting for his students, turn it into a kind of Shakespearean play. It was only later, after we were married, that I learned he was personally struggling with these issues. The first years of our marriage were a joy. My husband was a warm, gentle man, who cherished our two little boys. We lived in a duplex apartment near the college, surrounded by ancient forests. We often took the boys on long walks through the woods. He would scoop up one boy at a time, hug him and place him on his shoulders. As far as religion went, we would occasionally attend a Unitarian-Universalist service. But most often, he would bury himself in ancient religious texts. He kept saying to me. 'I must find the true meaning of our existence, our purpose.'"

Ginsberg was fascinated by her story, and watched her expressions closely as she spoke. "One day my husband told me he was going on a pilgrimage. No one could come. He needed to be alone. Nearly a month later, he came back with a badly broken leg. He wasn't the same, and gradually I began to lose him. He gave up his academic work. We moved back to his hometown of Stuarton, and inherited his father's real estate business. He grew distant from me and the children. Then, one morning, he told me that he had found the true meaning for his life. The Devil had chosen him as his agent in the endless struggle between good and evil. He told me I must go before he hurt me—that our children had been spiritually divided as well. One child was to be like his father, the other like me. He wanted a divorce. At first I said no, but I soon realized that I was married to a man who no longer could love me or even touch me. I agreed to the divorce. I took the younger boy. He took the older one. I couldn't make it as a single mother. There just wasn't enough time to make a living and take care of a child. I finally turned my son over to his father."

"What was your husband's name?" asked Ginsberg.

"Rufus Bideau."

36
Showdown Time

Brody Brady emailed the members of The Martini Club calling them to an emergency meeting at his place—no martinis or hors d'oeuvres, just serious business. They were assembled within an hour.

"I have some terrible news," Brady began. "We have been scammed—fooled by Rufus Bideau. Verde Bioenergy is not coming to Stuarton. There are no negotiations to build a switchgrass plant here and never have been. Rufus Bideau simply made the whole thing up to get us to overpay for a worthless farm."

Brady was pale. He stretched his frail body to its full height, and in a deep, sorrowful voice added, "And I was his messenger, his fool. He evidently saw how I had been duped by the New Universal Trade Center group and that little stripper girl. He sought me out. Somehow, I will make this up to you, my friends. I will see that all those who joined The Burning Bush Investment Club are reimbursed."

"Fat chance," snarled Gerald Smyth.

"None of us had to invest a dime," Ginsberg interjected. "We are all grown men capable of making financial decisions on our own. We can't simply blame Brody for our bad judgment."

"Maybe we can turn the farm into an airstrip for senior citizens," joked Jay Corrigan, the retired airline pilot. "I always wanted to give flying lessons to old people. Bring them closer to heaven, so to speak." He laughed, trying to break the mood.

"Right," Smyth shot back with his trademark sarcastic anger. "Maybe we could invest in a fleet of small airplanes with built-in porta potties. You know how us old folks always have to pee. Better yet, we could sell tickets to watch you wing walk, Corrigan…or maybe I should just kick your smart ass all over the room for fun."

Corrigan, who had flown F14 Tomcats over Vietnam as a Navy fighter pilot, rose from his chair and headed toward Smyth. "I never backed off from your types before, and I'm not gonna do it now."

"Hold on. I may have a better solution, if we can all just stop panicking for a moment." David Neville stood up. "What if we could still make this switchgrass thing happen?" A thin man of average height, he was hardly an imposing figure, but he had served on President Johnson's Council of Economic Advisers and was respected by the club's members. "Not being as trusting as the rest of you, I recently put in a call to Verde Bioenergy's vice president for North American investments. Turns out, he's an old friend of mine. I told him we had heard the company was going to build a plant here. When he denied any knowledge of it, I suggested that Stuarton could offer terms as favorable as Victorton and that he should speak to our mayor. He asked me some questions, and said he would be in touch. In light of this glimmer of hope, I suggest we continue to show confidence to our fellow investors and tell them things are just going to take a little longer than we thought."

"That's not a bad idea, but it doesn't curtail my desire to break Bideau's neck first," said an even-angrier-than-usual Smyth.

"I know where Bideau's office is, but that enormous son of his, Lucas, is his receptionist," Brady jumped in, hoping to blunt Smyth's desire for retribution.

"Bullshit," snapped Smyth. "I'm going there right now. Anybody coming with me?"

Mike Rose whipped open his jacket, revealing his pistol. "I'm with you."

"Never thought I'd have a brothel owner for backup, but now's the time," Smyth answered with a half smile.

"I don't endorse violence," Ginsberg said, "but as Koheleth said, 'There is a time for peace and time for war.' I'm coming along."

Corrigan and Brady quickly agreed to join the retired CIA agent as well, Brady announcing that he would drive. Neville said he would stay behind with an open phone line, so reinforcements could be called in, if needed.

Smyth gave the remaining members his dark look and followed Brady, Rose, Ginsberg and Corrigan out to Brady's car.

37
Confrontation

AFTER RECEIVING LONGCASTLE'S call, Sheriff Elijah Pew decided the time had come to bring in Rufus and Lucas Bideau for questioning. He was ready to charge them with the murder of Caleb Lampkin. Pew considered the scenarios that might await him. Rufus was a businessman and likely would stay calm, cooperate with the authorities and demand to speak to his lawyer. Lucas was another matter. He had a reputation for violence among bar owners across the state. Pew picked up the phone and ordered two deputies to follow him in a second squad car. The backup made him feel more comfortable as he drove toward Rufus Bideau's office.

Pew had passed Bideau's office building many times, but not learned the name of its owner until now. His research told him that this ramshackle structure dated back to the 1920s, when Rufus's grandfather, Samuel Bideau, a businessman and part-time missionary, had it constructed to serve as the headquarters for both his activities. Rufus's father, Eli, eventually took over and focused mainly on real estate, leaving religious good works to his dad. Rufus, at first, chose to be a scholar, majoring in religious studies in California. He returned when Eli died and became one of the most ruthless businessmen in Stuarton's history.

The sign inside the entrance read RB&S Corp. Underneath, the formal name was spelled out—Rufus Bideau & Sons—Lucas and Chris Bideau. Office on second floor.

The sheriff and his deputies swiftly climbed the stairs. Sitting at a desk just beyond the stairs was Lucas Bideau. A computer stood on a stand to his left. Country music blared from a radio sitting on a nearby shelf. Lucas was reading a magazine called *The Male Thing*.

"Whadda you want?" he said, without looking up.

"I'm Sheriff Elijah Pew. These are my deputies. I'm here to see you and your father, Rufus Bideau."

Lucas finally took his eyes away from the topless, buxom woman featured on one of the magazine's full color spreads. He stared at the badge on Pew's chest then up at his chiseled face. Their eyes met. "My daddy's not here, and I don't want to talk to you, so leave."

The sheriff looked at the seated Lucas. "Is that your father's office down the hall?" he growled and started passed the reception desk, the deputies following.

Lucas dropped the magazine, stood up and blocked Pew's way. He was six inches taller than the sheriff and fifty pounds heavier, most of it muscle. He stared down at Pew. "What do you want us for?"

"Questioning in the murder of Caleb Lampkin."

In one swift motion, Lucas seized Pew by the shirt and hurled him into the two deputies. All three law-enforcement officers were slammed against the wall. Bert Tompkins, the smallest of the three, fell sideways, banged his head on a coat rack and slumped to the floor unconscious. Pew and Deputy Malcolm Jarvis landed next to Tompkins in a tangle. Shaking off the impact, the sheriff reached for his weapon. But Lucas was on him, wrestling the pistol away. Pew rolled sideways. Tammy Wynette's country music almost blended with the crack of Lucas's first shot. The bullet struck Jarvis above his protective vest, lodging near his throat. The deputy gasped, as blood spouted from his wound.

Lucas pivoted to shoot the sheriff but found his wrist locked in a steel grip.

"No," screamed Chris Bideau, who had rushed in after the first shot. "Drop the damn gun, Lucas."

Unable to break his brother's iron grip, Lucas switched the weapon to his left hand, swiftly turned and shot his brother in the forehead. Chris fell to the ground dead, his eyes open wide in disbelief.

"I told you daddy said I'd finish you one day," Lucas hissed, looking down briefly at Chris without emotion. He turned back to finish off the sheriff, who was pulling out the backup pistol holstered above his ankle.

Too slow, flashed through Pew's mind as he struggled to get the pistol into firing position. *It's over*. But a fraction of a second before Lucas could pull the trigger, he was struck hard by two swift blows, one to the back of his neck, the other to the wrist, forcing him to drop the gun. Crazed with pain and anger, Lucas spun toward his new attacker, seizing him around the waist. Gerald Smyth grunted with pain but managed to drive the palm of his right hand against the base of Lucas's nose, forcing the hard cartilage up into Lucas's brain. Simultaneously, Smyth scraped the side of his shoe down Lucas's shinbone. Lucas moaned loudly, and released Smyth who toppled to the floor.

Blood streaming from his mouth and nose, a wounded and furious Lucas lurched toward Smyth. Two bullets from Mike Rose's pistol stopped him. One struck Lucas in the head, the other passed through his chest. He crashed to the floor dead. Rose had been a step behind Smyth as they had raced up the stairs.

Rufus Bideau had ordered Chris to rush to his brother's aid when the first shot rang out. They had been hard at work on a plan to acquire a nearby golf course that was up for sale. When the shooting continued, Rufus pulled a revolver from his desk drawer and rushed to the hallway in time to see Rose shoot Lucas. He then glimpsed Chris's body on the floor.

"You killed my boys," he shrieked. "You killed my boys!" He fired his gun at Rose, striking him in the arm and knocking him down. Sheriff Pew shot back. The bullets struck Rufus Bideau in the arm and gut, the second near his heart. Rufus staggered backwards waving his revolver from one person to the next, as if uncertain whom to shoot. He could see the sheriff and his deputies on the floor along with Rose. The others he recognized as members of The Martini Club. Bideau crashed back against the frame of his office door and fell inside. He kicked the door closed.

"First man through that door takes a bullet," he shouted. "Why'd you have to kill my boys? We could have talked about this."

"Lucas killed Chris," Ginsberg shouted. "And Lucas was killed in self-defense."

"Like Cain and Abel, rabbi?" Rufus managed. "But Cain lived and prospered, damn it. He didn't die on the floor of his father's office." There was a momentary silence. Smyth, the rabbi and Rose wondered if Bideau had died.

Then, in a gurgling voice, the man who had duped The Martini Club began to speak: "And the Lord said, 'Whosoever slayeth Cain, vengeance shall be taken on him seven fold.' Lucas should have been given his chance. Now, you will all burn in Hell...where I'll be waiting for you."

"Lucas gave us no choice," the rabbi responded from down the hall. In the distance, sirens wailed as ambulances and police responded to calls about shots fired and officers down.

"Rabbi," Rufus Bideau wheezed in the loudest voice he could muster. "Come in. We have to talk. I won't shoot."

Ginsberg started forward, but Smyth grabbed his arm. "Are you crazy? He'll shoot you dead the moment you enter. Lies roll off his tongue."

"I have to take that chance," the rabbi replied.

"He's a black-hearted son-of-a-bitch who doesn't care who he hurts—or kills," the retired CIA man warned.

"Listen to him," Sheriff Pew joined in. "Don't put yourself in danger. He's already killed Caleb Lampkin."

"Gerald, you and the sheriff are good men, but there is a dying man in there who needs to talk to me before he goes. For my own reasons, I must talk to him as well."

With that, Nathan Ginsberg walked down the corridor, opened Bideau's office door and walked in.

38
A Theological Discussion

RUFUS BIDEAU CRAWLED back from the door and propped himself up against the back wall of his office. A plaque thanking him for his contributions to Goodness of God College hung directly above him.

"Come in and kneel beside me, rabbi" Rufus said, waving his gun in the direction of the floor. "You don't look like much of a clergyman to me, with your turtleneck sweater and sporty jacket."

"Clothes don't make the man," Ginsberg said as he knelt.

"What does make the man, rabbi? His education? His professional success? His doing for others?"

"All of the above, and a lot more," Ginsberg answered, keeping his voice calm.

"Like sleeping with my ex-wife?" Bideau offered with a hard smile.

Ginsberg's eyes widened. He had not expected this. "I only learned yesterday that Mary was once married to you."

"Is she still a good lay?" Bideau went on. "She was so hot, so passionate. She would cry when I stopped humping her and plead for more. I had some women in my day, rabbi, but she was the hottest. What do you think, Mr. Clergyman, Mr. Rabbi."

Ginsberg knew he was being baited. "I walked through that door because of Mary. She would want someone with you now because she is that kind of human being."

"So you came in here so you can tell her that you comforted me as I was about to die? I see. Makes sense. This way, you won't have any of that famed Jewish guilt next time you fuck my ex-wife. Good thinking, rabbi."

"You are a no-good, son-of-a bitch who just shot one of my friends. You scammed me and a whole bunch of good people. You treated the whole world, including your wife and children, like crap. You are pure evil, Rufus Bideau." Ginsberg could no longer conceal his rage. "You deserve to die, and, in truth, I want to bear witness."

"My, my. That from a man of cloth," Bideau managed, feeling himself growing weaker. "I'm glad you did not come here to comfort me in my last moments. Perhaps you would like to drive a stake through my heart instead?" Bideau began to chuckle, then coughed violently as blood continued to fill his lungs.

"I don't know how to give comfort to pure evil," Ginsberg continued. "It pains me to see any human die, but someone like you deserves death. You tormented Mary for years. Because of you, your two boys are dead! They were murdered as much by your hand as anyone else's. You swindled me and my friends, but that's the least of it. That was only money. The sheriff says you murdered that poor farmer who owned the land you sold us. You took a life for mere greed. You are a monster."

"That farmer was a worthless old drunk. He was a means to an end, nothing more. Perhaps I overestimated your intelligence, rabbi," Bideau continued. "You should be smart enough to know it wasn't about the money. It was about the game—ripping off your little gang of has-beens. It was about making them wince with pain and realize how stupid age has made them. Yes, I take pleasure in making all of this come to pass."

The throbbing pain in Bideau's chest was making it more and more difficult to breath. He waved his revolver at Ginsberg's face. "I could kill you now, rabbi," he rasped, "but you are worth a bit of amusement, so I'll reserve that pleasure. I'd like to hear more from you. You surprise me. I had expected only bleating prayers from a keeper of the lambs." Bideau spit blood and winced. He waited for the pain to pass. It did not.

"You are so naïve about life and God," Bideau continued, "but you have some intelligence. I'll grant you that. Let us have a nice, final theological talk. Then we will both die, and perhaps continue our conversation in a more perfect place."

Ginsberg talked himself out of wrestling the pistol away from Bideau, who was clearly very close to death. The rabbi needed to buy some time. "Then you need me, if not for comfort, then as a kind of confessor."

"Confessor? No, never. You shall be my student, rabbi. Mary may have told you, I have studied many religions. I finally found one that made sense of the world. In my religion, evil is an essential mechanism of life here on earth. So you see, the evil I have done has not been for its own sake. I am the instrument of a higher power seeking to achieve a greater purpose."

Ginsberg stared intensely at Bideau, pretending to be interested in his rant. In fact, he was assessing Bideau's decline. Inside, the rabbi's blood was boiling, but he knew his life depended on Bideau believing he was engaged in his philosophizing.

Bideau rambled on. "As one of the great English poets said, there cannot be 'a blank and cloistered virtue.' Goodness needs an adversary, and evil plays that role. I used to believe in predestination—that a panoply of gods determined our fate. No more. I learned that evil allows us the opportunity to choose in the hope of finding virtue. It is a struggle without end. I gave you and your greedy friends the opportunity to make a choice. You chose poorly. As a result, the farmer and my two sons are dead. But the choice had to be made. You see, rabbi, it is our choices that define us. They are the only truth."

Ginsberg forced himself to remain collected. On the inside, his entire being was shaking. "You cannot hide your sins behind a philosopher's logic, Rufus. My God is not the product of rationality. He is the product of my faith. My God is a responsive God, not subject to inevitable laws. He is the creator of those laws, and only He can do away with them. As humans, we cannot always understand Him, but we can always talk to Him and feel His presence. We have made Him in our image, so we can understand something of His greatness. In return, He has made it plain to us that we have always had the right to choose. Adam and Eve in Genesis made the first choice when they ate the forbidden fruit of the tree. We never needed men like you to offer us temptation."

Bideau uttered a weak laugh. "Didn't Eve need the serpent?"

"The serpent was temptation, but the choice was hers. Eve gave us knowledge...end of story."

"Yes, end of story. I am tired of our conversation, rabbi. I am dying." Rufus Bideau called upon his last ounce of strength to raise his pistol. He pointed it at Ginsberg and fired.

39
Clean Up

SHERIFF PEW AND Gerald Smyth crashed through the door together. Rufus Bideau's head was slumped on his chest.

"What happened?" the sheriff asked. "We thought we'd find you dead."

"I don't really know," Ginsberg answered. "He raised his gun to shoot me, but it fell just as he fired. The bullet missed me and struck the wall."

They turned. A bullet hole had torn through the wallpaper next to the framed photograph of a woman. Ginsberg recognized her immediately. It was his Mary. So, there still was some humanity in him, he thought.

"Another couple of inches, and he would have blown your head off," Smyth said. "You were nuts to come in here and damn lucky you can walk out."

"I'm not sure I can," Ginsberg chuckled. "My legs are a little shaky."

"When you feel better, I'm going to want a full statement, rabbi," the sheriff said, "as well as one from you Mr. Smyth, and everyone else who came to Bideau's office with you. One of them, that Mike Rose fellow, went to the hospital along with one of my deputies. Another guy was found lying on the stairs leading up here. He's dead, but not from a bullet wound. My guess is he had a heart attack. The coroner will know for sure."

"Who?" the rabbi asked.

"His driver's license says Brody Brady. He lived over in Parrot's Caw. Funny, that was one of Rufus Bideau's big investments," Pew answered.

"Did they take him away yet?" asked Ginsberg.

"Afraid he's headed to the morgue, rabbi."

"I will join him there and offer my prayers."

"Damn," muttered Smyth. "I liked that snake-oil salesman, even if he cost me a bundle."

Crime scene investigators were moving around the office now. Smyth and Ginsberg said they would go to the sheriff's office as soon as possible to give their statements.

Pew grabbed Ginsberg's arm before he could leave. "Rabbi, what did you and Bideau talk about?"

The rabbi hesitated for a moment. "I'm really not sure—something about his religious beliefs."

40
Nathan and Mary Grieve

Several hours went by before Nathan Ginsberg composed himself, and could talk to Mary. How could he tell her that he had witnessed the deaths of her two sons and ex-husband? He finally decided it would be best to call her before going to see her.

"Mary, it's Nathan."

She was sobbing uncontrollably. "I already know. The police were here. They told me Chris and Lucas are dead...and Rufus. Oh my, God! My sons are both gone!"

"Can I come over?" he asked, holding back tears and feeling devastated by her distress. Then, more quietly, he asked, "Did they tell you I was there?"

"Yes," she answered in a frozen voice.

He was at her front door in less than fifteen minutes. For the first time, Ginsberg noticed how small and modest Mary 's apartment was. Inexpensive furniture—the kind you buy at a big box store and put together when it arrives—was complemented by cheap impressionist reproductions hanging on the walls. Standing on an unpretentious étagère was a photograph of Mary with two young boys, perhaps eight and ten. It was an image of happier times with her sons Lucas and Chris.

He watched her from across the room. He was afraid to touch her. Sitting on the couch, she looked like a fragile China doll that might break in his hands.

"Nathan," she sobbed. "My family is gone. I have nothing left!"

"You have me," Ginsberg offered, his voice cracking. She extended her arms, and he rushed to embrace her.

"The police said I have to go to the morgue and identify the bodies. I'm not sure I can do that alone. Will you come with me?" Ginsberg nodded. There was a long silence between them as they found comfort in each other's embrace. "Nathan, tell me what happened—what really happened." Her voice faltered, and they both struggled to hold back tears.

"Of course," he began quietly. "I will tell you what I know, but I'm afraid my story will be incomplete. Everything happened so quickly. It all seems so unreal now. A few men from a group I'm in called The Martini Club went to Rufus's office after we learned he'd swindled us out of some money. As we started up the stairs, we heard gunshots and yelling. The rest is a bit confusing, Mary, and may be hurtful to you. Are you sure you want me to continue?"

"Yes, please," Mary whispered, dabbing at her eyes with a small lace handkerchief.

"When we reached the top of the landing, we saw people on the floor. Lucas was about to shoot the sheriff, but my friend, Gerald Smyth, intervened. Lucas threw Gerald to the floor and went after him. At that point, Mike Rose, another member of The Martini Club, pulled out his gun and shot Lucas. He died instantly. I am sorry, Mary. You can take comfort in the fact that he did not suffer."

Mary slumped over with grief and began weeping more deeply. Ginsberg looked down, finding it difficult to continue. "There is no easy way to tell you the next part of the story, Mary. One of the people lying dead on the floor was Chris. The sheriff told us Lucas shot him. Apparently, Chris tried to stop his brother from killing everyone in the room."

Mary stared at Nathan through wet, glazed eyes, trying to understand this catastrophe beyond comprehension. "Lucas killed Chris?" There was a long pause as she tried to process how such an unfathomable question had become a true statement. "It had to be his father," she said angrily. "Lucas would only do this for Rufus. He idolized that bastard."

Other motivations raced through Nathan Ginsberg's mind, like the biblical hatred of older brothers for their younger siblings. He just shrugged and said, "I don't know."

Mary stood and wiped her face. "I think I should go to the morgue now. Will you drive me?"

Ginsberg nodded. "You didn't ask me about Rufus. I was with him when he died. If it is of any comfort, Rufus talked of you in his last moments. I think somewhere, deep down, he still loved you."

41
Brody Brady's Farewell

Brody Brady's funeral mass reflected the man. The jovial priest at the Holy Communion Church said the appropriate prayers, and noted with a smile that Brady's attendance at Sunday services was at best sporadic, and his desire for confession nonexistent. The Martini Club members and others in attendance chuckled quietly. "Brody Brady was a man who was touched by God in many ways," the priest continued. "He was filled with joy, humor and love of life. He was generous to a fault, always paying an extra tithe to the church. On that terrible day of his death, he was rushing to aid his friends when his fragile heart gave out. No more could be asked of any man."

Staring out from an open casket, Brady seemed to be smiling at the small audience—a former wife, a few distant relatives and several women whose connection to Brady was unknown, at least to the members of The Martini Club. Brady had no children.

After the burial, the club members adjourned to the home of David Neville. Though retired, he had agreed to handle Brady's legal affairs, putting to use his many years of professional expertise as a lawyer. Earlier in the day, Neville had read the will to family members who shared equitably in Brady's small estate.

His second ex-wife wept in surprise. She thought she would get nothing, she said, because Brady never had much money to begin with.

After the relatives left, Neville brought in the remaining nine members of The Martini Club, filled a Martini glass for each of them and began a toast to their late friend. "He led us down some strange paths, but he made us laugh every step of the way." Glasses were raised as everyone smiled. "But I also know you are concerned that we, our families and friends are out one million dollars because of his persuasiveness."

Mike Rose, his left arm in a sling, interrupted. "He also owes me more than a thousand bucks in hospital bills for getting me shot by that psycho." The men laughed.

"There you go again," said Smyth sarcastically. "Just when I was going to thank you for saving my ass, you go into this Jewish thing about money."

As if on cue, Rose opened his jacket to reveal his holstered weapon. "Just one more word from you Smyth. Just one more word."

"You really are one tough, little son-of-a-bitch," Smyth smiled. "I'd be honored to have you in the foxhole with me, any time." He walked over to Rose and gave him a bear hug.

"If I may continue," Neville said. "I've taken the liberty of contacting Verde Bioenergy, which, believe it or not, has expressed interest in coming to Stuarton some time in the future. First, they want to see how the Victorton plant works out, but I think this is hopeful news."

"I'll be dead by then," moaned Corrigan. "Maybe I can get a job around here crop dusting, assuming there are any crops to dust. Or, like I said, maybe we can turn our farm into a flight training school for old farts. It would be a great investment, if any of us had any money left to invest."

"Wait," Neville objected. "I have not yet finished. Brody came to me after he talked us into investing. He said he had some concerns about the project and could not bear to have his friends 'burned' by Burning Bush. He told me that many years ago he'd taken out a one-million-dollar life insurance policy, which named his first wife as its beneficiary. When she died recently, he changed the beneficiary to the members of The Martini Club. Since there are nine of us, each will receive more than one hundred thousand dollars. Presumably, we will use this money to reimburse all those whom we convinced to buy memberships in Burning Bush."

There was a stunned silence. Then Smyth shouted, "Say the prayer, rabbi. We all need a drink."

"Hear, hear," the members shouted.

Nathan Ginsberg bowed slightly toward his friends. "I will be happy to say the prayer, but first I'd like to invite you all to my forthcoming marriage to Mary Latham."

A second cheer went up.

"Now say the damn prayer before I let Rose shoot you!" Smyth yelled. Everyone laughed.

The rabbi nodded and began. "Baruch atah Adonai…"

To learn more about Alan Eysen, visit alaneysen.com.